TOO YOUNG TO DIE

Maybe she should explore her feelings for her family and friends, Melissa thought. Of how much she cared about them and of how precious they'd become during her illness. And what about life once she got out of the hospital? Would she be normal again? Who would ask her for a date? Who would ever kiss her or want her? Melissa sighed and thumbed through the blank pages. *Sixteen is too young to die*, she thought. She tossed the book aside, knowing that she had a lot to say and no earthly idea of how to say it.

TOO YOUNG
TO DIE

Lurlene McDaniel

BANTAM BOOKS
NEW YORK · TORONTO · LONDON · SYDNEY · AUCKLAND

RL 4, IL age 10 and up

TOO YOUNG TO DIE
A Bantam Book / August 1989

The Starfire logo is a registered trademark of Bantam Books,
a division of Bantam Doubleday Dell Publishing Group, Inc.
Registered in U.S. Patent and Trademark Office and elsewhere.

*Scripture quotations marked (NIV) are from the Holy Bible,
New International Version. Copyright © 1973, 1978, 1984
by International Bible Society. Used by permission of Zondervan
Bible Publishers.*

All rights reserved.
Copyright © 1989 by Lurlene McDaniel.
Cover art copyright © 1989 by Karen Kolada.
No part of this book may be reproduced or transmitted
in any form or by any means, electronic or mechanical,
including photocopying, recording, or by any information
storage and retrieval system, without permission in writing from
the publisher.
For information address: Bantam Books.

If you purchased this book without a cover you should be aware
that this book is stolen property. It was reported as "unsold and
destroyed" to the publisher and neither the author nor the
publisher has received any payment for this "stripped book."

ISBN 0-553-28008-2

Published simultaneously in the United States and Canada

Bantam Books are published by Bantam Books, a division
of Bantam Doubleday Dell Publishing Group, Inc. Its trademark, consisting of the words "Bantam Books" and the
portrayal of a rooster, is Registered in U.S. Patent and
Trademark Office and in other countries. Marca Registrada.
Bantam Books, 1540 Broadway, New York, New York
10036.

PRINTED IN THE UNITED STATES OF AMERICA

O   15   14   13   12   11   10   9

For my sons, Sean and Erik

"Not only so, but we also rejoice in our sufferings, because we know that suffering produces perseverance; perseverance, character; and character, hope. And hope does not disappoint us . . ."

ROMANS 5: 3–5a (NIV)

TOO YOUNG
TO DIE

Chapter One

"Melissa. Melissa Austin, are you awake?"

Melissa groaned at the sound of her name being whispered with repeated pokes in her side. She opened her eyes wide enough to see that her bedroom was still shrouded in darkness—pitch black darkness. What could Jory possibly want at this hour of the morning?

"Go away . . ." she muttered. Her arms and legs felt like lead weights, her brain foggy and disoriented. Every joint in her body ached.

Jory persevered. "But it's four A.M. Aren't we going with Michael as his spotters?"

It came back to Melissa in tiny spurts. Michael, her brother. Hot-air ballooning, his favorite sport. Jory Delaney, spending the night in order to drive Michael's pickup truck as his chase vehicle while he maneuvered his balloon into the Florida sunrise above. "It can't be four o'clock already. We only just went to sleep!"

"Correction," Jory said. "*You* fell asleep the minute you hit the bed. *I've* been up all night waiting for this."

Naturally Jory would be anxious, Melissa thought as she struggled again to clear her head from the cobwebs of sleep. She wished she felt better. "You've got to get over this fixation on my brother," she grumbled,

1

more annoyed at having to get up so early than with
Jory. "He's twenty and you're sixteen—just like me.
He's a sophomore at the junior college. You're a junior
in high school—just like me. He's . . ."

". . . waiting for us in the kitchen. So get a move
on," Jory directed, ignoring the facts that Melissa
pointed out. "If Michael asked me to push peanuts
with my nose on the streets of downtown Tampa, I'd
do it. Remember Romeo and Juliet. Princess Di and
Prince Charles. We're only talking four years here."

Jory flipped on the overhead light, and Melissa
felt as if her eyeballs had been pricked with pins. She
swung her legs over the side of her bed, stood, and
almost fell over.

"Whoa. You okay?" Jory asked, already tugging on
her jeans.

"Of course I'm okay," Melissa lied, feeling light-
headed. "Just a little wobbly from lack of sleep." She
ambled to her dresser and rummaged for jeans and a
T-shirt, dragging her thick, straight, black hair out of
her eyes. She had one leg in her jeans when Jory said,
"Melissa, you're bleeding."

Sure enough, blood trickled down her tanned leg
from below the knee. "Oh, I must've cut it when I
shaved my legs last night."

"And it's still bleeding? You'd have thought it
would have clotted by now."

"Could you hand me a tissue and that roll of tape?
I don't think there are any more gauze bandages left."

Melissa wiped off the trail of blood and secured
the tissue over the cut. It did seem odd that it was still
bleeding hours later. She forgot the cut as she dabbed
on blusher and lipstick and decided she should buy a
concealer stick for the dark circles under her eyes.

"Are you coming?" Jory asked impatiently from

the doorway. "In lieu of a toothbrush, how about a mint? We've got to go!"

Melissa clasped her waist-length hair back and followed Jory into the kitchen where Michael was already waiting. "I thought I was going to have to wake you two myself," he muttered. "I've made coffee for the thermos and there's granola bars in the cupboard. Let's get going." He was dressed in well-worn jeans, and his black hair was still damp from a shower, all five foot ten of him smelling of clean, fresh soap.

"Sorry," Melissa said, catching the keys that he tossed for his pickup truck.

"I'll ride in the back with the balloon. We've got twenty minutes to get to the field and meet the others."

Melissa sensed Jory's disappointment. "Why don't you drive?" she suggested to Michael. "We can all crowd into the cab."

Michael turned his sapphire-blue eyes toward her. Sometimes looking at him was like looking into a mirror. He had the same square face, high, angular cheekbones, and dark eyebrows as she. "All right," he said. "At least I drive faster than you." Jory flashed Melissa a glance that screamed *thank you*!

Outside the dark morning was humid and heavy. Melissa walked around Jory's new white convertible, running her hands along the gleaming paint covetously. The three of them squeezed into the cab of Michael's beat-up truck, and Melissa waved Jory in first, making certain she was wedged in the middle.

Michael sipped coffee from a Styrofoam cup, driving with one wrist draped over the steering wheel. "Are you meeting in the usual place?" Melissa asked.

"The usual." It was a cow pasture in the northwest corner of the county.

"Is ballooning fun?" Jory asked.

"There's absolutely nothing like it," Michael told her. "It's hard to describe. There's nothing but sky and wind and the whoosh of the gas jets. I suppose it's as close to heaven as some of us will ever get."

"Maybe you could take Jory up sometime," Melissa ventured.

Michael laughed. "I took you up, and how did you repay my gesture?"

"So I'm afraid of heights and got sick to my stomach." Melissa defended herself indignantly. "It could have happened to anyone."

"I've been skiing in Aspen and water-jetting in the Bahamas, but I've never been ballooning," Jory offered. "I've got a stomach like a rock, and heights don't bother me."

Melissa smiled at Jory's hints, but she wished Jory hadn't mentioned her many adventures. Rich girls put Michael off, and he probably thought she was boasting. Not that Jory was snobby. It wasn't her fault she'd been blessed with a wealthy family.

"I think you're better off staying on the ground," Michael said evasively.

He turned the truck off the road and it bounced through pasture land. Suddenly the headlights glared on a group of people clustered in the field. Several wore shirts stamped "Blue Sky Balloon Club." Michael halted, pulled on the hand brake, and stepped out onto the spongy sod while Melissa and Jory tagged behind. Someone said, "We almost started without you, Austin. Sun's due to rise in half an hour."

"My spotters overslept," he said, dragging his balloon off the truckbed. The lightweight nylon fluttered while Melissa helped him spread it out on the ground apart from the other balloons. Propane tanks hissed hot air into the necks of the dormant balloons, and they rose slowly like giant mushrooms. As each one filled, a person climbed into the dangling basket while others released ropes and the balloons drifted upward, like colorful bubbles in the sky. Michael leaped into his basket, and Melissa watched as the ropes were loosened and the mammoth balloon floated up through the gray morning mist.

"I'd have given my eyeteeth if he'd taken me," Jory said with a sigh.

"Maybe some other time." Melissa consoled her gently. Why couldn't Michael be sensitive to Jory's feelings for him? "Come on." She took Jory's arm. "Now *our* job starts."

In the truck, Melissa drove across the bumpy terrain toward the road. "Don't let him out of your sight. When he sets it down, we have to be there to help him pack it up."

"Seems like a lot of hassle for such a short ride to watch the sunrise."

"He loves it. And I'm glad he got into it. If Michael isn't working either of his jobs, he's going to school. Mom worries about him—she thinks he works too hard for his own good. But my brother's *very* determined to succeed."

"He isn't the only one," Jory said, pouring a cup of coffee and shooting Melissa a sidelong glance. "You've had your nose in a book ever since school started two weeks ago. You haven't even taken time to do anything fun with me lately."

"Don't be selfish, Jory. The PSATs are coming up in October and I've got to score big if I'm going to be eligible for a National Merit Scholarship next year."

"Do you still have your hopes set on Princeton?"

"If it's good enough for Brooke Shields . . ." Jory

giggled. But Melissa added, "Seriously, I don't want to be stuck at a junior college like Michael. I want to go somewhere new, do something productive and meaningful with my life."

"Does that mean law?"

"Probably. But I'm keeping an open mind." She glanced over at Jory. Her auburn bangs hung shaggy over her carefully plucked eyebrows. Her pert, turned-up nose gave her a sassy look brightened by almond-shaped sea-green eyes. Jory appeared to wear a perpetual pout, but her frequent dimpled smiles softened her face. Melissa considered her best friend seriously. She was pretty, rich, and smart to boot. "You could come to Princeton, too, if you concentrated on studying instead of boys and partying."

"Ugh." Jory wrinkled her nose. "One genius in this friendship is enough. I'll be your manager."

"Lawyers don't need managers."

"All right, your social director. Surely you plan to *date* between spurts of studying."

"There's really no one I'm interested in." Melissa felt color creep up her neck, and her conscience nagged, *except Brad Kessing*. Blond. Athletic. Bright. A senior. And absolutely unobtainable. Melissa knew what the most popular kids at Lincoln High thought of her—she was "bookish" and "pretty but intellectual."

"And why not? Gosh, Melissa, have a little self-confidence. Look at yourself: gorgeous black hair down your back, huge blue eyes, legs that start at your neckline, and brains coming out of your ears. You could have any guy at Lincoln you set your mind on."

"My mind's on college, Jory. That's my number-one priority. Are you watching Michael's balloon?" Melissa deftly changed the subject.

The sky was streaked with color, melting from indigo into pale lavender, laced with fingers of pink. Jory rose up on her knees and stretched the upper half of her body out of the window of the cab. "I see him! He's pretty high up and heading east." The wind caught her words and flung them back.

"Drat!" Melissa eased over into the traffic, looking for the first road that turned left. "If he's high up, that means there are power lines. Don't lose sight of him." She found a road and turned, caught sight of the balloon in her windshield, and accelerated. A sharp pain shot through her knee and she winced.

"Are you all right?" Jory asked, sliding back into her seat.

"Just my rheumatism acting up," she joked. "Now tell me why you won't come to Princeton with me? Your grandfather will send you anywhere you want to go."

"You said it yourself, Melissa—I'm a party girl. Princeton's too staid and proper for me. Besides, someone has to stay behind and keep an eye on your brother."

Melissa rolled her eyes. "You're impossible! Stick with guys our own age."

"They're absolute children."

By now the sun was up and the light through the windshield pierced Melissa's eyes.

"I think he's coming down," Jory said, pointing to the red-and-yellow balloon drifting down toward an empty field.

"Terrific," Melissa grumbled. "How am I going to get through the barbed wire?"

"There's a gate." Jory pointed excitedly.

Melissa drove the truck through the gate and then headed across the vast green pasture, where

Michael's balloon squatted, already deflating and fluttering in the breeze like a sailboat.

"God, that was great!" Michael shouted as the girls climbed out of the truck to help him fold the giant arch of nylon and put it back on the truck. His blue eyes shone and his face was flushed.

"He's high," Melissa teased, her words doubled with meaning.

"It's incredible—high above the earth, seeing the world like a bird does. Man, it's almost better than—" He caught himself, glancing self-consciously at Jory.

"Better than sex?" Melissa finished drolly, quoting one of his frequently used descriptive phrases. "I wouldn't know."

"You better not." He grinned. "Now let's get moving and I'll treat everybody to breakfast."

Melissa laughed and reached to unlatch the back of the truck. She stared down at an ugly purple bruise on her arm. Now how in the world had she gotten that, she wondered. She ignored it and dropped the tailgate with a bang.

"Don't break it," Michael chided. "It's not much, but it's paid for."

"Sorry. I lost my grip."

They crowded into the cab and Michael headed back across the field toward town. Jory chattered in a stream of quick, witty observations about ballooning and Michael's passion for it. Melissa dropped her head against the seat and watched the cloudless blue sky shoot past, her eyelids growing heavy. She wished she weren't so tired. But it was good to be alive. Good to breathe in the fresh, warm September air.

Lulled by the movement of the truck and the

warm sun, Melissa felt content. Her junior year of high school would be her best, and her gràdes would be her highest. She'd make sure of it. The course of her future depended on it.

Chapter Two

"You didn't have to be so rude to Jory, Michael," Melissa said testily the minute they walked into the kitchen of their house and Jory had driven off in her convertible.

"Rude? What are you talking about?" Michael lowered himself into a chair, stretched out his long legs, and clasped his hands behind his head. "I thought I was very tolerant under the circumstances."

"What circumstances?"

"She's a bubblehead."

Melissa felt her anger rise. "She's my best friend and has been since the fifth grade."

"She's also rich and spoiled. Why does she hang around here anyway? And why does she go to Lincoln High when she could go to any private school in the city?"

Melissa answered his second question first. "She goes to Lincoln because she likes public school. A lot of kids prefer Lincoln to private schools." *Like Brad Kessing*, she reminded herself. For although he traveled in Jory's charmed circle of monied elite, he too preferred Lincoln. "And she hangs around here because she has a crummy home life."

"And ours is perfect?" There was an undertone of bitterness in his question that made Melissa sigh.

She sat across from him at the table and fiddled

10

with the salt shaker. "I didn't say it was perfect. Face it, Michael, Dad's been gone six years and he's not coming back. *I* think Mom's done a terrific job of keeping us together, don't you?"

He nodded. "Mom's a great lady. But she works too hard."

"That's what she says about you."

A small smile started at the corners of his mouth. "That's because I'm going to be rich someday, just like Miss Delaney. Then Mom won't ever have to go downtown to the office again. And she won't have to worry about paying bills and trying to make ends meet."

"You know it's not that bad since she's gotten her promotion. And besides, you're missing the point. Jory has money and two parents but she's not particularly happy, and that's why she likes to come over here. We may not have much money, but at least we're a family. I think Jory senses the closeness between us and wants to be a part of it." Melissa paused, remembering the times over the years that Jory had come home from school with her. She'd stay as late as she could, until Mom had to drive her home to an often dark and empty house in the exclusive neighborhood of mansions where she lived.

"Her parents are always off chasing real estate deals, and Jory's left alone. Her older brothers and sisters all live in other states, and none of them are close to her anyway. I mean, not like you and I are."

"She's not always alone," Michael said with a twinkle in his eye. "She's usually over here."

"Oh you!" Melissa flung the salt shaker at him, exasperated.

"Now don't tell me you aren't just a tiny bit envious of her," Michael said. "I see the way you look at her car. Wouldn't you like to have someone hand you the keys to a machine like that, absolutely free?"

"I didn't say money isn't important. I said it doesn't buy happiness."

Michael leaned across the table and tugged affectionately on her hair. "Ah, the idealism of a sixteen-year-old! What I'd give to have it again."

Melissa lunged at him and he laughed, catching her wrist. She grimaced as his fingers closed around her bruise. He dropped her arm and eyed the ugly purple mark in surprise. "What's that? And how did you get it?"

"Just a bruise, and I don't know." She was curious about her bruises too, but couldn't figure out how she got them. "Probably stumbling around in the dark at four A.M.," she said, poking Michael lightly in the arm.

"Does it hurt?"

"It's a little sore, but it'll go away." Unable to divert his look of concern, she teased, "You know how we princesses are. Just a pea under our mattress and we turn black and blue."

Michael stood and stretched, his physique rippling with muscle. "I think I'm gonna crash for a couple of hours before I go to work. Tell Mom not to count on me for supper. I'm working overtime at the warehouse shelving stock. We get paid double time on Saturdays you know."

"You don't *have* to work so hard for your money," Melissa said, the light of mischief in her eyes.

"How's that?"

"You could always marry it."

Michael shook his head in amusement. "And I'll bet you can fix me up with just the right rich girl."

"In a few years." Melissa smiled. "She's much too young for you now."

"You're a hopeless romantic, Sis."

"And you're a hopeless pragmatic."

"I tell you what, when you get that law degree, I'll hire you to run my empire."

She stuck out her tongue, and he bounded out of the kitchen with a laugh.

On Monday, Jory picked Melissa up for school. Melissa decided it wasn't a bad way to arrive each day—in a sporty white convertible with plush red interior. After Jory's second tour of the parking lot, Melissa asked, "Is there some reason we're cruising and not parking?"

"Absolutely. We want to be seen, don't we? How can we march straight into the building without first making sure that everyone at Lincoln is totally aware of our arrival?" To emphasize her point, Jory waved at a group of students congregated in the lot. Behind them, Lincoln High rose, an ultramodern glass and concrete structure, only two years old and already nearly filled to capacity. Yellow buses unloaded at the far end of the parking lot, and Melissa was glad she didn't have to be on one.

"When you're finished cruising, could you please park? I need to get to homeroom early," Melissa said. "On Friday, Mr. Marshall said he wanted to see me first thing today."

"Ugh." Jory wrinkled her nose. "What a way to start the week. Well, it can't be anything you've done wrong—everyone knows Melissa Austin is the model student."

Jory slowed and honked. Melissa glanced in the

direction her friend waved, and her heart suddenly somersaulted into her throat. Brad Kessing stood next to his bronze Firebird, dressed in khaki slacks and a sky-blue cotton shirt that accentuated his athletic build. The sunlight highlighted his golden blond hair.

"Hey, Brad," Jory called.

Melissa started fidgeting around in her purse for her hairbrush, and her nervousness must have caught Jory's attention. "What's the matter?" she asked.

"I just noticed that I look a mess. My hair's got a mind of its own today and—"

"Melissa, do you have a thing for Brad?"

"Oh, he's all right."

"All right?" Jory mused. "Then how come you're turning three shades of red?"

"I am not!"

"Are too!"

Melissa settled pleading eyes on her friend. "Just keep it to yourself, okay?"

"Why? I can introduce you two. Brad and I go way back. Our parents play doubles at the country club all the time."

"Just drop it," Melissa demanded, speaking under her breath, even as Brad sauntered over to Jory's car and leaned his elbows against the door frame. "Hi, Jory. What's up?"

"Nothing much. Do you know my friend, Melissa Austin?"

Brad's cool blue eyes took her in, and Melissa's mouth went dry. The strong lines of his jaw and chin etched themselves into her brain. "Hey, Melissa."

She managed a nod before Jory blurted, "Are you playing in the club tournament next Saturday?"

"Not this time. The soccer coach wants us to take

t easy so we don't get injured before practice starts for
he season. How about you?"

"Me—tennis?" Jory wrinkled her nose. "That *is*
he game with the racket and the little fuzzy ball, isn't
t?"

Brad laughed. "You're some athlete, Delaney."
His attention turned to Melissa. "Do you know any
nore about sports than she does?"

"I play racquetball with my brother every now
and then, but that's about as athletic as I get."

Brad scrutinized her, studying her features one
by one while her stomach fluttered. "Maybe Jory
could bring you out to the club sometime and we
could knock a few balls around."

"Maybe."

"Just name a time," Jory said. Melissa could have
killed her. From far away, a bell sounded. The spell
was broken and Brad straightened, breaking his hold
on Melissa's gaze. He tapped the side of the car.
"Maybe I'll see you two around later."

As he ambled across the parking lot, Jory called,
"Count on it!"

"That was *so* embarrassing, Jory," Melissa hissed.
"Why didn't you just ask him to take me out on a
date?"

Jory snapped her fingers. "Why didn't I think of
that?" She maneuvered her car into a space that was
too small. "I told you I wanted to be your social director."

"Well, I don't need a social director. I want to
keep my mind on studying, because I'm going to get a
scholarship. I haven't got time for guys this year." She
opened the door and banged the side of the car next to
Jory's. "Now how am I supposed to get out?"

"Simple," Jory said with a smile. "Climb over."
She had already stood on the seat and swung her legs
to the asphalt below. Melissa followed, and as she sat
on the edge of the door she caught Jory staring wide-
eyed at her legs, which were blotched with large purple bruises. "What happened to you?" Jory asked.

Melissa felt a sharp pain in her knees and ankle
joints when she hit the pavement. "Nothing. And
don't try to change the subject. You practically threw
me at Brad. He must think I'm a real jerk."

"Oh, honestly, Melissa. You know what your
problem is?"

"No. But I'm sure you're going to tell me."

"You're too serious. These are supposed to be the
best years of our lives. You should be dating, partying,
having fun . . ."

"I know exactly what I want. And a boyfriend is
low priority." She limped slightly as she caught up
with Jory.

"Well, I *do* want a boyfriend," Jory said. "And if I
can't have the one I really want—"

"Michael?"

Jory cut her a sideways look. "—then I'll become
experienced enough to appeal to him in the future. In
the meantime, though, it's the party life for me. Do
yourself a favor, Melissa, and go after Brad before he
gets snatched up by some ditzy sophomore."

Melissa shook her head. Jory would never understand. Melissa wanted to take the world head-on. Like
Michael, she wanted things from life, things that college and hard work could bring her. Life was more
than an endless round of parties and days spent at the
country club. Romanticism aside, Melissa knew she
had a pragmatic streak, too.

She said goodbye to Jory and promised to meet

her at the car after school. Late for her meeting with Mr. Marshall, she rushed toward homeroom shrugging off a nagging fatigue, and when she swung into the doorway Mr. Marshall smiled at her.

"Good to see you, Melissa. Come closer. I want to ask you something." She approached his desk and he tossed aside his pencil.

"You're a very bright girl and doing far above average work. How would you like to come out for Brain Bowl this year?"

Chapter Three

"Brain Bowl?"

"Surely you're aware of the countywide Brain Bowl competition. It's a chance for the brightest students from each high school to come together and test their knowledge against each other in a team setting."

Melissa did know about Brain Bowl. She'd watched some of the finalist matches the previous spring on Tampa's educational TV channel. "I know it's a tough game."

"True. After county competitions, there are state. Even nationals."

Melissa shifted her notebook to her hip, her interest piqued by Mr. Marshall's words. "There're prizes, aren't there?"

The teacher pushed his glasses higher on his nose and smiled. "Big prizes. For the county winners, a trip to Washington, D.C., a thousand dollars in savings bonds to each panelist, and two thousand for the school. But for the state winners, it's a trip to Europe and a four-year scholarship."

Melissa's eyes narrowed. "But I thought only seniors were allowed to participate."

"Usually. But we need to have juniors primed for next year's competition. Since Lincoln High is so new, we didn't do very well in our last two outings. But this year, it's going to be different."

"How?"

His grin was broad and reminded Melissa of a little boy's. "Mrs. Watson and I are in charge. The preliminary rounds don't start until March, but we believe that if we start working now, we'll have a shot at putting the best possible team out there. Interested?"

Melissa nodded emphatically. She was very interested. "What Mrs. Watson and I did was to go through all the achievement scores for every one of Lincoln's juniors and seniors. We've based our selections on IQ and grade point average. You're high on both."

She felt deep satisfaction from knowing her hard work was paying off. She'd have to tell Jory the next time they got into a discussion about her studious habits. Mr. Marshall picked up a file folder and flipped through it. "However, being smart isn't enough in Brain Bowl. You also need a certain aggressiveness—" he gestured with a fist, "—a special presence when the heat's on you to come up with an answer."

"How do I try out for the team?"

"It's a multistage process," Mr. Marshall told her. "Next week we're testing all the kids whom we've already weeded out as having the academic potential. There will be a battery of tests after school for two days. They'll be academic, of course, with some psychological testing. We'll need parental consent for you to take the tests." He reached into the folder and handed her a form. "If you score in the range we need, you'll begin Brain Bowl drills three days a week during sixth-period study hall, and then probably every day after school until the competition begins.

"We won't choose the final team—four panelists and two alternates—until a month before the competitions. Then we'll *really* hit the drilling hard. Proba-

bly every day, so there won't be much time for
anything else. Especially a social life." His eyes
drifted. "My wife threatened divorce if I got involved
in Brain Bowl again this year, but there's something
about the event. You get sort of swept up in it." He
grinned with satisfaction. "Anyway, you should realize
that you may work for months and still not be selected
for the final team. But we're not restricting the panel
to seniors. We're going after the right chemistry, the
right mix of talent. We want to win!" He paused. "For
the Green and Gold, of course."

Lincoln's colors. "Of course." By now, homeroom
was filled, and Melissa had to take her seat. "I'll get
my mother to sign the form, Mr. Marshall. I'd like to
be eligible for the selection."

He flashed her another smile. "I thought you
might. You're a good student. And Mrs. Watson thinks
you're team material."

Melissa had had Mrs. Watson the year before for
advanced English and had earned an *A*. She walked to
her seat with her head spinning. Brain Bowl. A four-
year scholarship. At the least, a savings bond. She
wanted to make it. Inwardly she smiled, feeling a rush
of confidence mingled with joy. *Princeton.* Maybe it
wasn't such a pipe dream after all.

That night she helped her mother make a salad.
It was just the two of them since Michael had classes.
Melissa related every word of her conversation with
Mr. Marshall to her mother. "I've got the form in my
room," she said. "You will sign it, won't you?"

Mrs. Austin, a tall, slim woman with dark hair,
listened intently. Melissa felt her mother's eyes on
her. "Is that the way you want to spend your junior

year? Studying after school almost every day? Without
any guarantees you'll make the team?"

"I want to go to college."

Her mother sighed. "How did I ever raise such
success-oriented kids? All I wanted to do when I was
your age was get married."

"I want it all, Mom. Lots of women have careers
and families. Why can't I do both? *You* do."

"I *had* to," her mother reminded her. "I would
have been perfectly content to stay at home and raise
babies. But, when I did have to go to work, it would
have been much easier if I'd had an education to fall
back on. As it was, I started at the bottom."

Melissa remembered. After her husband had
walked out, Janelle Austin had started with the phone
company as an operator on the night shift, even
though it meant leaving fourteen-year-old Michael in
charge at home. Melissa had learned to rely on
Michael and to feel safe with him guarding the
doors—Michael and his baseball bat would fight off
any intruder! For a while they had been strapped fi-
nancially, but they'd made it. And they'd made it with
enough style that Jory Delaney, the cute little rich girl
in Melissa's fifth-grade class, spent every available moment at the Austin household.

"Michael wants to be wealthy enough so that
you'll never have to work again," Melissa said over the
sound of running water as she washed vegetables.

"That's very kind and noble of him. But I'd probably work now even if I didn't have to. Once the two of
you are out on your own I'll have little else to do."

Melissa felt a certain sense of pity for her mother.
Alone. That's how she was facing the rest of her life.
Sometimes Melissa wondered why she had never re-

married. She was still pretty. Perhaps her clothes were a bit dated. . . . Melissa shot her mother a glance. Did she still miss their father? Still long for him? The image of Brad's clear blue eyes floated into Melissa's memory. A girl could easily lose her perspective and allow herself to get lost in them. She jerked herself away from the seductive daydream. No. She'd made up her mind. Studies came first from now on. The Brad Kessings in her life would simply have to wait. She refused to travel the same road her mother had.

A sudden, sharp pain in her fingers caused her to drop the vegetable peeler with a noisy clank.

"Goodness. What happened?" her mother asked.

Gingerly Melissa flexed her fingers. "Just a cramp," she said. But it had been more than that— more like a deep aching inside her joints. Maybe her crack to Jory about rheumatism wasn't so far off the mark.

A rap sounded on the back door. "Well, hello, Jory," Mrs. Austin said, smiling.

"Am I interrupting supper?"

"We haven't started yet."

"Then I'll come back later."

"I wouldn't think of it. Come in."

Jory shrugged at Melissa self-consciously. Her auburn curls were streaked with hair paint, and her outfit was straight out of a fashion magazine. Melissa was sure it had cost a fortune. "I—uh—was just driving by." Melissa waved her over to the sink.

"You know you don't need an excuse to stop in, Jory," Melissa's mother said, taking salad plates out of the cupboard.

"It's just that my parents are at the club tonight. Some sort of charity auction. The house felt lonesome . . ." Her sentence trailed and she shifted from foot to foot.

"Have you eaten?"

"Uh—sort of."

"For Jory, 'sort of' means a Coke and a bag of chips."

"Coke and chocolate chip cookies," Jory corrected with a smile that crinkled her eyes and revealed her dimples.

"We're only having chef's salad, but you're welcome to join us."

"Michael's at school tonight," Melissa added, conveying information in a way that only Jory would understand.

"I'd love to stay," Jory said, acknowledging Melissa's message and Mrs. Austin's invitation with gratitude. "I've always *loved* your chef's salad."

"Here." Melissa handed Jory three glasses. "There's ice tea in the fridge. You'll have to work for your supper."

"Small price," Jory said while opening the freezer door to get ice.

They sat at the kitchen table eating and talking. It often amazed Melissa how much Jory could talk. Afterward Jory shooed Mrs. Austin out while she and Melissa cleared the table and stacked dishes in the dishwasher. "So you're going out for Brain Bowl?"

"Sure am."

"Guess I'll have to find something to get involved with then," Jory said.

"You could test," Melissa urged. "I know you're very smart."

Jory rolled her eyes. "Pul-eez. I couldn't walk in the door with my grade point average. No, you go on without me. You're the one who wants to go to Princeton."

Melissa nodded. Although she hated to admit it, Jory had brains, but no initiative. "I haven't made it yet," she said.

"You will. Hey! Why don't you plan on spending next Friday night with me?" Jory asked with a quick turn of her body. "The testing will be over by then, and my folks will be on a cruise to the Bahamas. We can rent a ton of VCR movies, stay up all night, and pig out on pizza."

Melissa considered the offer. "You won't make me sit through *Aliens* again, will you?"

"You mean that touching story about monsters wrapping humans in cocoons for future meals? Naw."

"Some comedies this time, all right?"

"We'll go to the rental store together, and you can pick out any ones you want. I'll put it on Daddy's tab." Her smile was impish. "Then we'll take off Saturday morning for the country club—go swimming, have lunch, do the sauna. I'll put that on Daddy's tab too."

Melissa flicked water in Jory's face. "You're impossible!"

"What else are rich parents good for?"

To help send you to college, Melissa thought. How could Jory be so casual about her future?

Melissa hung back in the girls' room until the very last minute on the afternoon of the test. She nervously dropped her hairbrush while running it through her hair for the umpteenth time. She noticed her face in the mirror looked gaunt, and dark circles smudged the skin beneath her eyes. She needed to get more rest, she thought, so she wouldn't look like a raccoon.

Melissa adjusted her blouse and noticed another purplish blotch on her arm. "Oh, good grief," she said to her reflection. Not another bruise. Melissa didn't know what was causing them, but she did know she had to do something about them. Why, just the other day she'd caught her phys ed teacher staring at the bruises on her legs. "Leg makeup," she mumbled in a sudden flash of inspiration. She'd buy leg makeup to hide them. Dancers used that trick all the time.

Pushing the bruise problem to the back of her mind, Melissa tried to focus on the situation at hand. *The test*. At the testing room she paused, wondering how many people would be inside. Would she know anyone else? It's probably a roomful of nerds with IQs in the extraterrestrial range, she told herself. *What chance have I got?*

The room was surprisingly crowded, and she did recognize many faces. *Shocking to find out who's really smart,* she mused. Melissa looked around for an empty chair. Suddenly, her gaze stopped short and her stomach lurched as Brad Kessing flashed her a dazzling, heart-thudding grin.

Chapter Four

Melissa felt herself blush. She nodded briskly at Brad's smile and hurried past him to an open desk in the very back of the room. Of all the kids at Lincoln, Brad Kessing was the last she had expected to see sitting in the room. *Well, why not?* her mind argued. She'd heard that he was smart. She only wished that seeing him hadn't rattled her so. Why had it? Why, when she'd vowed not to be distracted by boys this year in pursuit of her academic goals?

You're being ridiculous, she told herself with annoyance. *You don't have time for infatuations.*

For that's all it was. Brad simply had the right blend of looks and charm that appealed to her.

Melissa's thoughts were interrupted as Mr. Marshall came in and tried to quiet the restless group of students assembled in the room. "Good afternoon," he began, dropping a stack of papers on the desk in front of him. "Mrs. Watson will be here shortly, but I want to get you started." He surveyed the room with a broad grin. "Do you realize that your cumulative IQs rank up in the same numerical category as the national debt?"

Giggles twittered and feet shuffled. "As Mrs. Watson and I have told each of you during the past few days, it is our goal that Lincoln put together the best combination of talent and skill for the countywide

Brain Bowl competitions. It's not just brains we're looking for, but self-confidence, openness, an ability to think quickly on your feet . . ."

Mr. Marshall's voice trailed off as Mrs. Watson, a small-boned woman who moved with economical, determined purpose, entered the room. She had black hair, and features that were sharp and angular. Her brown eyes were studious, seeming to miss nothing. As she surveyed the room, kids sat up straighter and became subdued. She said, "I'm glad to see so many of you here. Today's test is a quest for knowledge. We've compiled the questions from actual Brain Bowl questionnaires. Tomorrow's test will gauge emotional and psychological factors."

A student quipped, "You mean, it'll tell you if any of us are crazy geniuses?"

"We already know *that*," Mr. Marshall joked. "The tests will tell us who's able to sit under the interrogator's eye without flinching." He rolled his hands together like a mad-scientist and caused another ripple of giggles through the audience.

Melissa listened intently, determined to score high in every area. Mrs. Watson continued. "From these tests, we'll whittle the group down to twenty-five people whom we'll interview and pare down to ten finalists. The group of finalists will be decided quickly—I'd say within two weeks. That panel of ten will drill together, study together, and work side by side until April, when we'll choose six final panelists to begin the preliminary rounds of Brain Bowl. After that initial round-robin—since I *know* Lincoln will still be in it"—a smattering of applause broke out— "we will advance to All-County—which will be televised, I might add—and from there to State finals."

A hush fell over the room as the meaning of Brain

Bowl suddenly became real to each student. Then Mr. Marshall asked, "Any questions?" There were none, so he passed through the rows and lay the tests face-down on each desk. Mr. Marshall returned to the front of the room and announced, "Let the games begin."

Melissa took a deep breath, mumbled a quick prayer, and began.

"Did you ace it?" Jory asked through a mouthful of pizza as she sat on her living room floor the following Friday night.

Melissa shrugged but offered a satisfied grin. "I didn't flunk. Actually, I knew more than I thought I would. And the psychological part was a breeze. I gather from the questionnaire that I'm socially well adjusted."

Jory gave Melissa a teasing look. "But how can that be when you had every opportunity to linger and talk with Brad Kessing after the tests and instead chose to zip away the minute they were over?"

Melissa gasped. "Who told you that?"

"Brad, of course. He asked me if you were attached or if you just didn't like him."

Flustered and embarrassed, Melissa was at a momentary loss for words. The truth was, she'd been too much of a coward to talk to Brad. He made her feel off balance and out of sorts. She was attracted to him but resisted it. "What's not to like?" Melissa asked nonchalantly. "I knew I was coming over here to spend the night and had a million things to do before I could come."

Jory rolled her eyes in feigned tolerance. "Well, I defended you staunchly, so you still have a shot at him. I told him you were probably preoccupied, since you had your heart set on making that brainy team. He understood."

Melissa wished Jory wouldn't be so helpful. What did she have to say to make her friend understand that she was committed to matters of the mind and not the heart? She scanned the living room with its Louis XIV heirloom furniture, plush lemon-yellow carpet, porcelain knickknacks, and cut-crystal vases of silk flowers. It crossed her mind that maybe Jory recognized something that Melissa could not see—that she probably could focus on school and have a social life, too. And that maybe it was unreasonable for her to deny her feelings about Brad.

Her gaze returned to where Jory had set the pizza box on a gleaming fruitwood coffee table. A grease stain streaked the dull shine of the wood. "You're ruining your mother's table," she noted irritably.

Jory shrugged. "The maid will clean it tomorrow. Are we going to watch movies or blabber?"

"Which TV? The one in your room, the den, or the family room?" Melissa asked, knowing that the irony of the question would be lost on Jory. Didn't *every* house have three TVs?

Jory jumped up. "Family room. Come see how I've fixed us up."

Melissa tagged after her to a cavernous room with beamed ceilings. The carpet had been covered with down comforters and mounds of pillows. Bowls of fruit nestled amid the folds of satin softness. "What's this?" Melissa asked with genuine delight.

"A Turkish harem room, dummy. Like it?"

"It's dynamite."

"Thanks." Jory's pixie grin highlighted her dimples and made her green eyes shine. *Why wasn't*

Michael nuts for her? Melissa wondered. "I've even rounded up some sexy negligees." Jory held up two wisps of flowing nylon. "Siren Red or Ice Princess Blue?" She asked.

"I feel red," Melissa giggled, taking the scarlet fabric from her friend. In minutes, both girls had shed their clothing and wrapped themselves in the sheer lingerie. Melissa whirled, her hair rippling loose and free down her back. "This is positively sinful."

"Yeah. But isn't it fun?" Jory spun around too. "You know, you need to eat more pizza. You're losing weight."

"You know what they say: 'You can't be too rich or too thin,'" Melissa joked.

"I'm not kidding," Jory answered seriously. "You really have lost weight."

Melissa smoothed the filmy material over her flat stomach. "Do you think so?"

"I know so."

"Well, it's probably just the cut of the gown."

"No, I don't think so . . ."

Melissa grew flustered and a little self-conscious over Jory's comments. "Don't make such a big deal about it, Jory. Are we going to blabber or watch movies?"

Jory shrugged and began sorting through the pile of videocassettes they'd chosen earlier that afternoon from the video store. "What'll it be?"

Melissa flopped provocatively onto the sea of cushions and nibbled daintily on a cluster of grapes. "How about *Casablanca*? I feel romantic."

Jory shook her head and shuffled through the stack. "You're weird, girl. You want romance, but not with a real live willing and able guy!"

"Dreams take less energy than the real thing,"

Melissa said, as a sudden tiredness rushed through her. She stifled a yawn.

"You're not going to fall asleep on me like the last time you stayed over, are you?" Jory demanded with a cry.

"Absolutely not," Melissa said, even as her eyelids struggled to stay open. "Well, I may doze off, but nudge me for the scene in the fog, when Bogart and Bergman say goodbye."

Jory gave an exasperated sigh and stretched out next to Melissa on the fluffy floor coverings. "Some concubine you'd make," she grumbled. "Asleep before the sheik arrived."

Melissa managed a smile and drifted into a hazy world of lethargy. "When the prince comes, have him give me a kiss."

"What if he's a frog and gives you warts?"

"Then I'll defend him. He has a right to an attorney." The last thing she remembered was Jory's squeal of exaggerated distress as sleep overcame her.

The next morning, Melissa buried her face in the downy coverings, too tired to move, feeling as if she'd been drugged.

"Rise and shine," Jory directed from the far side of the room, balancing an ornate silver tray laden with doughnuts and Cokes. "Time for breakfast."

Melissa groaned. "What time is it?"

"Nine on the nose, and we have a full day ahead of us."

Melissa struggled up, raking her tousled hair from her eyes. She felt tired and achy. She hoped she wasn't coming down with the flu—not with so many great things going on in her life. She reached for a glazed doughnut. It tasted warm and sweet. "Delicious."

"I drove over to the bakery myself because I couldn't blast you awake. You missed some good movies," Jory added with a hint of accusation.

Sheepishly, Melissa shrugged. "Sorry. My eyes just refused to stay open. This past week must have been more strenuous than I thought."

"Yes. Deep thinking can be hazardous to your health."

Melissa pelted Jory with a fluffy pillow. "Well, I'm awake now. What's the game plan?"

"The country club, of course."

Melissa glanced toward the bank of high windows in the room. Sunlight slanted inward, in taut ribbons. "We can swim in your pool," she suggested, still feeling sluggish.

"Forget it! Get your suit on. We're leaving in thirty minutes. There's a certain lifeguard who's come to my attention . . ." She let the sentence trail suggestively.

"I told you to stick to guys at Lincoln."

"And I told you they're all children. I prefer older, more experienced men. Come on, let's move it."

In the bathroom, Melissa tugged on her bathing suit, then stepped into crisp white shorts and a gauzy blue cover-up. She twisted her thick black hair into a braid and secured it with a gold clip at the end. Finally, she smoothed on some waterproof leg makeup she'd bought. It had cost a fortune, but it did an excellent job of concealing those ugly bruises. The makeup had become a regular part of her dressing routine, though she'd forgotten to use it after gym class Friday, and she'd caught her teacher staring at her legs again. It was so embarrassing, she vowed to be more careful.

She daubed on lipstick and blusher and met Jory at the car.

Melissa lolled against the upholstery of Jory's convertible, watching the intense blue sky slip past overhead. Hot Florida sun beat down despite the early morning hour as the car wound its way through the wrought iron gates of the country club and along a winding driveway lined with oleander.

Jory stopped in the circular driveway before a massive stone-and-cypress building, where a valet opened their car doors. Melissa grabbed her duffel bag and followed Jory up the steps into the cool interior. Tropical flowers and pools of water graced a giant lobby domed by soaring ceilings and skylights. Tinted glass walls allowed sunlight to filter through to palm trees growing in cultivated garden boxes and hibiscus blooming in thick profusion. Jory elbowed Melissa. "Let's hit the pool first. We'll do the sauna and game rooms later."

Melissa needed no further urging. She longed to stretch out on a chaise lounge and drift lazily in a netherworld of near sleep while the sun browned her body.

The pool area wasn't crowded. Red striped umbrellas dipped over redwood tables on the deck. Melissa blinked against the reflection of bright sun on the calm water. "That's him," Jory whispered, pointing to a bronzed lifeguard perched in a special chair on the far side of the pool. "You'll excuse me while I go check out his availability?"

Melissa nodded, depositing her towel on a lounge and lying down on her stomach. "Don't let me cramp your style."

Jory paused and remarked wistfully, "I wish it were Michael."

"Maybe someday . . ." Melissa said consolingly and closed her eyes. The sun soaked through her. She barely heard the sounds of the splashing and laughing surrounding her. She might have gone to sleep, but a voice said, "Hello, Melissa."

She sat up, startled, and found herself face to face with Brad Kessing.

Chapter Five

"Hi," she said, as a surge of adrenaline chased away her sun-induced stupor.

"It's good to see you. Jory mentioned that you two might come out here today."

Jory. No wonder she'd insisted on coming to the country club. "You're not swimming?" she asked. Brad wore yellow jams and a tank top that showed off his tanned and powerful upper body. Mirrored sunglasses dangled from a cord around his neck.

"Just finished," he said. "I was thinking about playing racquetball, but I need a partner."

His look was an invitation. "I'd like to, but I'm a little low on energy," she told him, knowing she had neither the stamina nor the presence of mind to get through a game with him.

His blue eyes traveled the length of her, and she felt a tingling sensation that she associated with romance novels. "Want to go through the gardens in the back? There are ponds with goldfish a foot long."

She'd walked the gardens often with Jory, but to go there now with Brad. . . . She glanced at Jory, who was engrossed in conversation with two guys at the lifeguard station. She'd never miss her. "Sure. You lead the way."

As she slipped on her cover-up and sandals, Brad flipped her heavy braid, the tips of his fingers brush-

ing lightly over her shoulder. She followed him down a
flagstone path, and in minutes the pool area had disappeared. Silence settled around them in thickets of
green as they stepped into a tropical forest. Ficus
trees, crotons, and exotic shrubs were intertwined
with purple and fuchsia bougainvillea flowers. Brad
broke the intimate silence by asking, "How do you
think you did on the Brain Bowl testing?"

"I think I did all right. And you?"

His grin was lopsided. "I'm a Kessing. Kessings
always do all right. It's in the family rule book."

His comment was puzzling, but she didn't question it. "And I thought you were only interested in
soccer."

They stopped on a wooden bridge arched over a
winding stream where the water was green and still.
"Jocks aren't supposed to be smart. Is that what you
mean?" His question made her feel foolish.

"I didn't mean it the way it came out. I guess I
was just surprised when I walked into the room and
saw you in the front row." Her palms grew sweaty.
Nothing she was saying was coming out right.

"We jocks have reputations to maintain. I try not
to let on that I can think as well as I can kick a ball."
There was a hint of amusement in his words. "But I do
intend to make the Brain Bowl team."

She met his intense blue-eyed gaze steadily. "So
do I."

"Deep down I have a secret desire. I want to be a
Rhodes Scholar. Do you know what that is?"

He toyed with her braid, and her thoughts scattered. "It has something to do with athletics and academic achievements, doesn't it?" she said.

"Actually, it's a scholarship to Oxford University
in England. My grandfather was a Rhodes Scholar,

and I guess I've always wanted to follow in his footsteps."

Brad intrigued her. She'd never really known a guy who was interested in anything so profound and serious. Most boys she'd dated were only concerned with the latest football scores—or their own scores when it came to girls. But Brad was someone who really thought about his future. "I hope you get it," Melissa said with sincerity.

His smile was intimate as he said, "I always get what I go after." Melissa's heart hammered and her mouth went dry.

Brad rested his elbows on the rough wood of the bridge and leaned over, pointing toward the water. "Look, there's a fish." She caught a flash of gold as a fat, lazy fish ventured from beneath an overhanging rock. "Actually, they're carp, not goldfish."

Brad touched the nape of her neck and stroked her soft skin with his thumb. Melissa's knees turned weak and she leaned against the bridge railing for support. "Maybe that will be a Brain Bowl question," she said lamely, then told herself that it was a stupid thing to say.

"If we're on the team together, we'll be seeing a lot of each other."

His observation made blood pound in her temples. She didn't want this to be happening to her. "The team! I'm aiming for the first cut right now. I can't think beyond that."

"You'll make the first cut."

"How do you know?"

His smile was slow, confident. "Because *I'm* going to make the first cut. And I want you to come with me."

His sense of confidence momentarily overwhelmed her. He straightened and turned her to face him. "Melissa." His voice went low and quiet. "Can I unbraid your hair?"

Flustered by his request and change of subject she stammered. "Y-Yes. If you want."

He reached over her shoulder and pulled the tightly wound braid forward, unclasping the gold clip. She couldn't tear her eyes from his face, couldn't stop the emotions and sensations pouring through her body. Brad unwound the plait slowly, dragging his fingers through the thick, dark masses of her hair until the strands fell loose and free. He sifted it through his fingers like sand, gathering it into handfuls. A breeze spun wispy strands across her face. "God, you have beautiful hair." His whisper sounded worshipful.

Time stood still for her, in a rain forest of green and yellow, in eyes the color of the sky. Her breath pressed against her lungs, unable to escape. She managed to mumble, "Thank you."

Brad lifted a fistful of the dark tresses and let it fall, bit by bit, in a feathery cascade. When the last strands settled, he rested his hands on her shoulders. The thin, gauzy cloth of her shirt seemed nonexistent. He cleared his throat. "I'd like to get to know you better, Melissa. Maybe after the team's chosen . . ."

"Yes. Maybe."

He looked at the water below and a gathering of orange-and-white flecked fish. As he rambled on about the carp, she noticed that his arm never left her shoulder. And his fingers, long and gentle, never stopped stroking the dark veil of her satin, waist-length hair.

"You're awfully quiet. Didn't you have a good time?" Jory's words intruded into Melissa's brooding silence as they drove through the familiar streets of Melissa's neighborhood in the dusk.

"Of course I had a good time. The whirlpool and sauna were great."

Jory switched on her headlights. "But you're not telling me what happened in that hour you disappeared into the gardens with Brad."

If Melissa hadn't been so tired, she might have been irritated with Jory's probing. "Nothing happened. We went for a walk. We looked at the fish."

"You rebraided your hair when you came back to the pool area."

Melissa was relieved that Jory couldn't see the flush on her face because of the darkness. "It came undone."

Jory blew through her teeth skeptically, drove the car into Melissa's driveway, and shut off the engine. "It's okay to like Brad, you know," she said. "There's nothing wrong with balancing a social life with your studies."

"It seems that I don't have much choice," she admitted grudgingly. "He's very hard *not* to like."

Jory's smile was so obvious, Melissa could feel it in the dark interior of the car. "It's nice to know you're still human and that blue eyes and blond hair can still affect you."

"I'd have to be a corpse not to be affected."

Jory chuckled. "Well, under the circumstances, I'd say you were in for a banner year, Melissa Austin."

"*If* I make Brain Bowl," she cautioned. "I told you, studies come first with me this year."

"Okay. *If* you make Brain Bowl, and *if* you date Brad, will you confess that this could possibly be the best school year of your life?"

Melissa released an exasperated sigh. "I confess, Your Honor."

"Good," Jory said, opening the car door and jumping out. "Now let's go inside, where I can catch a glimpse of your gorgeous brother and make a fool of myself over him."

"You're impossible," Melissa laughed, climbing out of the car and heading to the door.

"True. But if I weren't, what would you do for comic relief?"

Melissa hugged her friend impetuously. "Study!" She entered the warm glow of her kitchen, where her mother had left a plate of homemade chocolate chip cookies on the table with a note saying, "Ran to the store. Be back in an hour."

Jory eyed the plate longingly, and Melissa read her thoughts just as surely as if she'd spoken them aloud. There would be no one back at her house. Her parents were still on their cruise. Nothing but a dark, lonely house that people passed through but rarely lived in. "Why don't you help me eat these?"

"You wouldn't mind? I mean, since there's no one home at my house, I could stay for a little while . . ."

Melissa pulled out a chair and shoved her friend into it. "Sit and eat. What kind of a friend would leave me alone to devour an entire plate of cookies just when I'm being noticed by the best-looking guy at Lincoln High? Do you want me to have to waddle up to the Brain Bowl podium?"

Jory reached for a cookie and munched it thoughtfully. "You *are* going to make the team, Melissa. I meant it when I said this is your year. Nothing can stand in your way."

Partly because of Jory's and Brad's enthusiasm, Melissa floated through the next several school days, and when Mr. Marshall told her of her selection to the initial group of twenty-five, she wasn't surprised. Three afternoons of playing the game convinced her that she was a good contestant. Brad was sensational, and by the following Friday, when Mr. Marshall and Mrs. Watson chose the ten finalists, Melissa's confidence buoyed her through morning until the list was posted on Mr. Marshall's bulletin board at noon. Melissa's name topped the list; Brad's was second. She barely read the others.

"I told you so," Brad said after stopping her in the hall between classes.

The fluttery sensation that she felt whenever she glimpsed him in the corridors churned in her stomach. "I never doubted it for a moment," she said.

His laugh was quick. *It certainly is going to be a banner year,* she reminded herself when he touched the heavy length of her hair with a casual, offhanded purpose. "I'll see you later."

Melissa was still floating on a cloud of happiness when, during seventh-period study hall, she was summoned to the dean of women's office. Curiosity dogged her down the hall to Mrs. Crane's cubicle.

The dean of women was friendly, blond, and stylishly dressed. "Have a seat, Melissa." She motioned to the chair beside her neat and orderly desk. "Congratulations on your selection to the Brain Bowl team. It's certainly the best one Lincoln's had to date."

"Thank you, Mrs. Crane." A slight case of jitters set in while the dean studied her for a few thoughtful moments, sweeping her with questioning, intelligent eyes.

"Have I done something wrong, Mrs. Crane?"

"Not at all."

Melissa began to grow wary, even apprehensive,

as the dean focused her attention on Melissa's long, graceful legs. Self-consciously, Melissa tucked one ankle behind the other and wished she'd worn jeans instead of a skirt. "I give up. What's wrong?"

"That's what I want you to tell me, Melissa."

Confusion blanketed Melissa's mind. "I don't understand. What do you want me to say?"

Mrs. Crane reached over and patted Melissa's hand as one might stroke a frightened child. "My dear, there are laws protecting children from parental abuse."

Melissa was dumbfounded. "E-Excuse me . . . ?"

The dean offered an indulgent, all-knowing half-smile. "The bruises on your legs have been reported, Melissa. You can tell me the truth. Is anyone hurting you at home?"

Chapter Six

Horrified, Melissa stared openmouthed at Mrs. Crane.

"Now, dear," the dean said, with a patronizing pat. "Please understand me. As a minor, you are protected by certain laws, and we school personnel only want to make sure that no one harms you. It's for your own good that I'm asking you to be honest with me."

Melissa's thoughts whirled and tumbled. *She thinks my mother beats me!* The impact of the thought sent blind rage coursing through her. A mental picture of her mother—bent over the kitchen table writing checks to pay a mountain of bills—flashed through her mind. In an instant, Melissa was on her feet. "Are you asking me if my mother hits me? No one in my house has ever struck me! No one!"

"Now, now, Melissa. Calm down. We can't ignore those bruises on your legs."

"I don't know how I got these stupid bruises. But they didn't come from my mother." Her anger was so intense that her teeth chattered. "There's some other reason for them."

"What other reason?"

Caught off guard, Melissa sputtered. "Maybe it's gym class. I don't know!"

Mrs. Crane refused to abandon her tack. "I can't let this go unreported, Melissa. I must call your mother in for a consultation. I would be negligent in my duties if I didn't."

"Don't you dare! My mother is wonderful. She'd never, *never*, strike me! You leave her alone."

"Melissa, please . . ."

Melissa didn't wait to hear what else the dean had to say. She bolted from the office and ran outside into the bright morning light. She shut her eyes in pain and felt dizzy as she ran through the parking lot, clutching her purse tightly. At the city bus stop she leaned against the bench for support.

Finally home, Melissa collapsed on her bed in tears and exhaustion. She knew she was skipping school and didn't care. She was so angry, she swore she'd never set foot in that school again.

Melissa snuggled into her covers, and when she woke the phone was ringing. Her mother's voice was anxious. "Melissa. Honey, are you all right?"

It took her a minute to clear her head and remember why she was home. "I'm all right, Mom."

"The school called. They said you ran away. I took the chance that you'd have the good sense to go home."

"I'm home. I'm okay . . ."

"Melissa, wait there for me. I'm leaving the office right now. I'll be there in twenty minutes."

"But . . . You don't have to leave. Everything's all right."

"Twenty minutes," her mother said urgently and hung up. Melissa washed her face, trying to pull herself together. She did feel lousy. What's wrong with me? she asked herself. She touched the glands in her neck and realized they were swollen. She couldn't get sick now—not with the start of school and Brain Bowl and . . .

When her mother arrived, Melissa slipped quietly into her arms, deeply comforted by the familiar hug. "Mrs. Crane told me what happened. We'll deal with her later. But now, let me see your legs."

Obediently, Melissa allowed her mother to examine her. "There really are a lot of bruises, honey. Are you sure you don't know how you got them?"

"No." Her body felt heavy, and all she wanted to do was lie in her mother's arms and go to sleep. "But let's not get so worked up over this, Mom. I've probably got the flu."

"I think you have a fever too. I'm calling Dr. Pace. I want him to check you over."

"I don't need to go see him, Mom. I'll take some aspirin and go to bed, and by tomorrow I'll be fine."

"This isn't a voting issue, Melissa. We're going to the doctor's." She smoothed Melissa's hair and forced a small smile. "Besides, I need vindication for the school. I can't let them think I beat my children into submission, now can I?"

Melissa shrugged. "I guess not," she said.

Dr. Pace's examination was routine. He checked Melissa with sure, confident fingers, feeling her swollen glands and bruises, then taking blood. She squeezed her eyes shut as the needle pricked her arm. "It's just the flu, isn't it, Dr. Pace?" she asked as he secured a bandage over the puncture in her vein. "I told Mom it's nothing but some flu that's going around."

His smile was professional, noncommittal. "It's something. We're just not sure what, yet."

"What do you *think* it is?" her mother asked uneasily. "I don't like the looks of all those bruises."

Melissa rolled her eyes, wishing her mother would ease off and that Dr. Pace would just send her home. "It could be as simple as anemia—that's common in girls Melissa's age," he said.

"Then I'll take iron pills," Melissa said, relieved

"Or, it could be mononucleosis." Dr. Pace peered at her over his glasses. "Which means you'll have to give up kissing."

She smiled at his attempt to cheer her. "No problem there. I've dedicated myself to studying this year Boys are out."

"Melissa made the Brain Bowl team," her mothe said, as if that might influence the doctor in some way

"I can go back to school, can't I?"

"I want to check a blood smear under my microscope. I'll be right back."

Melissa turned to her mother, who was sitting stiffly in her chair. "It's going to be all right, Mom," she said. Frankly, she was glad her mother had insisted on the checkup. She had been feeling bad for a long time, and deep within she had been concerned about it. If she was going to give Brain Bowl, and Brad, her best shot, she'd have to get better.

"Of course, you're going to be all right, honey. But I wish you'd told me about the bruises when they first appeared."

Dr. Pace returned, his expression unreadable. He positioned himself in front of her. "Your red blood count is low . . ."

Her smile was quick with relief. "Then just write me a prescription for iron pills and I'll take them faithfully. I promise."

He held up his hand. "Whoa. It's not that simple Melissa. Your white cell count, on the other hand, is rather high."

"So?"

"So I'd like to check you into the hospital for a few days of testing."

Melissa's heart almost stopped beating with the shock of his request. "The hospital!" Her mother echoed her words.

"Just for testing," he emphasized hastily.

"Why? I have school. I can't go to the hospital."

Dr. Pace took her hand. His was warm. Hers was cold. "Think of it as a vacation. You can bring your books. You'll even have a phone and a TV in your room—first-class accommodations at Hotel Tampa General."

"Is this absolutely necessary, Dr. Pace?" Her mother's voice sounded taut.

"Yes. It's important that we find out exactly what's ailing Melissa."

Melissa wanted to ask him what he was testing for, but she sensed he would not say. "When do I have to go, Dr. Pace?"

"The sooner the better. My receptionist will call and have your admitting papers prepared by this afternoon."

"So soon?"

"The sooner we get started, the sooner we'll know what we're fighting." Dr. Pace squeezed her hand. "Now, don't look so frightened. It's for your own good." He helped her off the examining table. She wanted to run out of the room screaming, but instead she offered a brave smile that in no way reflected the terror she was really feeling.

"Not bad, Melissa. Private room and everything." Tory toured her hospital room with an appraising eye. From the bed, Melissa watched her step carefully

around Michael, who was sitting in a chair near the
window, a worried scowl on his face. Through the
blinds, Tampa's evening sky glowed with the aura of
city lights.

"Want to take my place? All you can eat for only a
pint of blood a day."

Jory shivered at Melissa's ghoulish humor. It com
forted Melissa to have her friend pacing the room, for
her visit lent a sort of normalcy to an otherwise terri
ble day. Ever since Melissa had phoned her and Jory
had exploded with phrases such as "Nosy Mrs. Crane"
and "Are you all right?" and "I'll be there as soon as
visiting hours start," she had felt less alien in her anti
septic surroundings.

Only Michael's brooding countenance could pen
etrate the pretense of well-being Melissa had tried
hard to create. He hadn't been at all understanding
about her admission to the hospital for tests. Was he
just as afraid for her as Melissa was for herself?

"Brad asked about you today," Jory said. "I told
him you'd gone home sick. He says he hopes you get
well quick. The first full-fledged Brain Bowl drill
starts next week."

"Oh, they said these tests won't take more than a
few days." She propped herself against the pillow, al
lowing her dark hair to spread out in a fan on the crisp
white, starched linen. "Tomorrow they're doing a
bone marrow aspiration."

"Ugh!" Jory blurted. "Sounds yucky."

Melissa saw Jory's face redden as Michael shot
her a disgusted look. Instantly, Melissa felt sorry for
her, knowing firsthand the feeling of saying something
stupid in front of someone you want desperately to
impress. "Dr. Pace says it's not so bad if I get a good
technician."

"What are they going to do to you?" Michael asked.

"They take a sample of my bone marrow from inside my hip with a special syringe."

"They stick a needle into your bone?" Jory turned pale as Michael asked the question.

Melissa chewed her lip, anxious not to let on to Michael how scared she really felt. "It only takes a few seconds."

Through clenched teeth he said, "These guys had better not hurt you."

"Yeah, or I'll have my uncle in New Jersey fly down and break their legs," Jory announced.

Melissa tried to calm them both with a smile. "Hey, come on. I'm a big girl—I can take whatever they dish out. Besides, I'm too old to cry."

When visiting hours were over and Melissa was left alone, she plucked at the bed sheets, her bravado drowned in the hospital's night sounds that echoed around her. She *was* scared. And she *did* want to cry. Melissa felt overwhelmed with self-pity and helplessness. *Why is this happening to me?* Yesterday she'd been a normal sixteen-year-old girl on the verge of everything wonderful. Now she was hospitalized, and she was being poked and prodded, bled and taped.

She fought back the urge to weep, picking up her brush from the nightstand and absently running it through her hair. She remembered Brad's fingers, and she longed to savor his touch one more time.

"I'd heard from the nurses that there was a fox on the floor. They didn't lie." The male voice coming from her doorway startled Melissa so completely that the brush fell from her grip and clattered to the floor. In the doorway stood a stranger, surveying her with an insolent, wolfish grin.

Chapter Seven

Her surprise turned to anger as she stared at a tall, thin boy on crutches braced against the door frame. "Who are you, and what are you doing in my room?"

"My name's Ricter Davis. You can call me Ric. I have a room down the hall. What are you in for?"

Still startled, Melissa appraised him through angry eyes. He was at least her age, maybe older. His brown hair brushed his shoulders and his piercing brown eyes and lean, raw-boned features appeared arrogant. "Weren't you taught to knock before barging into somebody's room?"

"Hey, it's a free country, and besides, your door was open. I was watching you brush your hair, but you were in the twilight zone and didn't see me."

It annoyed her to think he'd been studying her without her knowing. She wanted to say something curt, to make him go away, but before she could he hobbled toward her on his crutches. Suddenly, she noticed that his left leg was severed below the knee. She tried not to stare, but her eyes seemed glued to the void where his leg should be.

"It's been amputated," he told her frankly, allowing shame and shock to collide inside her. Reaching the side of her bed, he added, "It's all right to stare. Everybody does."

"I . . . I didn't mean to. You just startled me."

"What's your name?"

"Melissa Austin." Did he have to stare so openly, so steadily at her?

"Why are you here?"

"Just tests. I'm having a bone marrow aspiration in the morning."

His expression never changed. "Too bad."

"Why? Why is it too bad? Does it hurt?"

"The test doesn't hurt as much as the results."

She sat up straighter against the pillows, uneasiness gripping her stomach. "What is that supposed to mean?"

He hesitated. "I'm sorry. I shouldn't have said that . . . I'm not sure what I meant . . . I really should get back to my room," he said faltering. "I'll stop by tomorrow, and we can talk."

Melissa searched for a tart answer, wanting to let him know that she wasn't interested in seeing him again. "Don't bother," was all she could manage.

Ric arched an eyebrow, turned on his crutches, and hobbled to the door. "Tomorrow," he said, and he disappeared. She listened to the squeak of the crutches' rubber tips fade in the darkness.

The technicians came for her early the next morning. Melissa forgot about her surprise visitor in her preoccupation with the tests. First, they did an electrocardiogram. "To rule out rheumatic fever," a man in a green lab coat told her, exposing her chest and sticking small metal disks to her skin. Wires from the disks led to a machine that scribbled on graph paper. "This gives us a picture of your heart's working condition."

"Rheumatic fever causes heart damage, doesn't

it?" As soon as she voiced the question, the thought frightened her. "What causes it?"

"Untreated strep."

Melissa swallowed against a scratchy throat. Could she have had strep throat and ignored it long enough to have caused rheumatic fever to develop?

The bone marrow aspiration was not so pleasant as the electrocardiogram. The nurse and technician were friendly, almost cheerful, making Melissa wary. They placed her on an examining table on her stomach, a pillow tucked under her pelvis. The nurse cleaned her hip area with iodine. The brown liquid felt cool and stained her creamy, white skin. Next she applied a cooling spray. "This is a local anesthetic, Melissa," the woman explained. "It will numb the site so you won't feel the needle going in. We'll insert it into the spongy part of the bone where your marrow is manufactured, and it won't take but a few seconds to withdraw the cells we need for lab analysis."

Melissa clutched the metal edge of the table, determined to focus her attention on the white tiled wall in front of her and not on the syringe that looked a foot long. She gritted her teeth as pressure, then pain, overcame her. It felt as if a vacuum cleaner were sucking out some of her insides. When it was over, the nurse gave her a perfunctory pat. "There. Now that wasn't so bad, was it?"

Yes, it was horrible. "No problem," she said as she blinked back tears.

"You'll be tender in that spot for a little while, but you can get up and walk around once you get back to your floor." The nurse settled Melissa in a wheelchair for the ride back to her room. "There's a video game machine up there if you're into Space Invaders."

But Melissa didn't want to socialize. She just

wanted to return to her room and study. Regardless of her hospital visit, she was determined to make a good showing in the Brain Bowl drill next week. Besides, studying let her escape from worrying about her mysterious illness.

Jory called at lunchtime. "Where are you?" Melissa asked.

"Drove over to McDonald's for lunch. I'm at the pay phone next door at the Seven-Eleven."

The familiar image of that corner, a hangout for Lincoln students, sprang so sharply into Melissa's mind that a lump came to her throat. "What'd you have to eat?" she asked, clearing her throat.

"The usual—Big Mac and large fries. You know my weakness for grease. Hold on—I have someone here who wants to say hi."

Sounds of the phone being fumbled and passed came through the receiver. "Hi, Melissa."

"Hi, Brad." Her voice went soft when she heard his.

"Jory tells me you're skipping school for a few days."

"Jory exaggerates. I'll be home in another day. I thought I'd experience firsthand the life of a laboratory rat. So far, it's not much fun, but it's given me a whole new respect for people who march for animal rights."

Brad chuckled. "Hey, did I ever tell you I'm glad you made the Brain Bowl team?"

"Yes, but not nearly in enough detail. I left school a bit suddenly the other day." She allowed the sarcasm to bleed into her inflection. "But you did predict at the country club we'd both make it. Are you psychic?"

"Just confident. And besides, didn't I say I wanted you on the team with me?"

Her pulse quickened. "Yes, you did."

"So hurry up and get out of that hospital. I wouldn't mind a few private study sessions between the two of us."

"I'll tell my doctor to put a rush on my case."

The phone passed back to Jory. "Well, I've gotta run. Chemistry lab next period, you know. Ugh. I hate it."

"Don't blow anything up."

"Ha-ha! I'll stop by to see you tonight. Do—uh—do you want me to bring a visitor?" Jory asked the question in a conspiratorial whisper.

"Don't you dare drag Brad up here, Jory Delaney! Do you hear me?"

"Just asking . . ." Jory huffed in mock innocence. "It's not every day you can legitimately have a guy ogle you while you're lying around in your nightgown. It could be kind of sexy."

"Forget it."

"I could bring the red harem gown . . ."

"*Jory!*"

"Suit yourself. See ya later."

Melissa hung up with an amused shake of her head. Jory was incorrigible. *Maybe that's why I like her so much,* Melissa thought. *Lucky, carefree, Jory. With nothing more serious on her mind than a chemistry lab.*

Michael popped his head around her door frame. "Up for some company?"

Delighted to see him, she lifted her arms for a hug. "I thought you were working this afternoon."

"I'm between jobs. Also, I have class tonight, and I didn't want to go an entire day without seeing you. Mom says she'll be up this evening. How are they treating you?" The lightness left his voice.

She rubbed her hip gingerly. "I've had better times in my life. But the sooner I get all this testing done, the sooner I can get back to a normal life."

He tugged affectionately on a hank of her hair. "You look pale."

"Michael, there is something I want to talk to you about."

"Name it."

Melissa fidgeted with her covers. "The money for all these tests. How's Mom gonna pay for all this? It isn't exactly built into our budget."

She saw his blue eyes, so like her own, take on a look of concern. "Mom has a good insurance policy. It'll pay for most of this."

"But we're talking about major bills. Even the balance after insurance pays its share will be hard to afford."

Michael tipped his head and smiled. "Why don't you read these fashion magazines Jory brought and stop worrying your pretty head about hospital bills?"

"Look, Michael, if I'm going to get that National Merit Scholarship I can't numb my brain with fluff about designer labels and the latest hairstyles."

"And you can't afford designer labels either," Michael teased.

"You're making fun of me," she snapped.

Michael hugged her and kissed her forehead. "Not at all, Melissa. I think you're beautiful. And brave, too. I'd kick somebody's face in if he tried to stick needles in *my* bones."

The blatant admiration in his voice made her own voice stick in her throat. "Don't be such a baby," she said, attempting to hide her embarrassment.

He laughed and kissed her goodbye.

Later that night, after her visitors had left, she

caught a glimpse of the boy Ric walking past her room. She quickly averted her eyes and held her breath, hoping he wouldn't follow through on his promise to visit her a second time. She didn't like him and she didn't want to know him. Luckily, he passed by without even glancing inside. She sighed and scooted down under her covers, wearied by the rounds of testing and the gaiety she felt compelled to show her visitors.

She hated to have her mother worry. Melissa was worried enough herself. She wanted out, wanted to go home and resume her regular schedule. They'd have some of the test results back by the morning, according to Dr. Pace. Until then, there was nothing for her to do but wait.

Two doctors came midmorning, while she was engrossed in her history book—Dr. Pace and Dr. Rowan, a bear-size man with bushy brown hair and large, strong hands. Behind them stood her mother and Michael. Melissa's surprise at seeing her family gave way to apprehension immediately. Her mother's face was pasty white.

"So many of you?" She gave a nervous twitter of a laugh. "Will it take two of you to hold me down for today's tests?"

Dr. Rowan said, "No more tests, Melissa."

"Mom? Why aren't you at work?"

"I wanted to be here when they talked to you, so I took the day off."

Fear tasted metallic in Melissa's dry mouth. She dipped her head, struggling to catch Michael's eyes, but he refused to meet hers. "Okay. So it's more than anemia." Why was her voice so high-pitched?

"Melissa, it isn't a common anemia. Or mono."

Dr. Rowan grasped her small hands, and she could feel the strength of his.

"Or rheumatic fever," she pronounced insightfully. Her gaze fastened onto the front of his lab coat, spotlessly white except for a faint brown stain on the pocket. She wondered if he knew that the pristine whiteness was marred by that single spot. "All right. I give up," she said, a bit too brightly. "What do I have?"

Dr. Rowan's unswerving gaze trapped hers and held it. "The diagnosis is lymphocytic leukemia, Melissa." His voice sounded clinical and very far away. "It's a form of cancer."

Chapter Eight

Melissa laughed. Dr. Rowan sounded absurd, and her family, hovering around her bed with stricken expressions, reminded Melissa of a silent movie. She quickly sobered and said, "I don't believe you. You must have made some mistake. I'm sixteen years old. How can I possibly have leukemia?"

Dr. Rowan gave her hands a slight squeeze. "The bone marrow aspiration confirmed it, Melissa. Leukemia is a blood disorder. It occurs when young white blood cells formed in the bone marrow reproduce abnormally and crowd out the normal ones. They take up the space of the red blood cells and the platelets. Platelets cause your blood to clot normally, and because your supply is low you've been bruising easily. Without enough red blood cells to carry oxygen, you become anemic. That's why you've been so tired all the time, and why you look pale."

Melissa only half heard him. She didn't care how many facts he produced to back up his diagnosis. She didn't believe him. "Maybe the tests were wrong." She withdrew her hands from his and folded them primly in her lap. "Tests can be wrong, can't they?"

"Sometimes. But not in your case."

Melissa glanced around him to her mother's face, where she saw the truth. "Oh Mom . . ."

Her mother wrapped her in her arms and held

her tightly. "We'll fight it, Melissa. You've got the best medical help available. And we'll fight it."

Dr. Rowan cleared his throat. "Medicine has made great advancements over the past few years in the treatment of different kinds of leukemia. Although we have no cure for the disease, we do have very sophisticated ways of dealing with it. The important thing now is to begin treatment as soon as possible."

"What kind of treatment?" Melissa's voice quavered as she asked the question.

"Traditional treatments include chemotherapy. That's when we bombard the leukemic cells with large doses of powerful cancer-fighting chemicals . . ."

"I know what chemo is," she snapped. "I read. I'm not stupid."

Dr. Rowan continued patiently. "Once we initiate chemo, we'll expect an improvement. It will take several days to establish the right combination of drugs, but our goal is to get you into remission as quickly as possible. Remission is a decrease, sometimes a reversal, of your symptoms. After we achieve remission, you'll go on to maintenance."

"Maintenance?"

"Yes. Once initial treatments do their job and healthy blood-forming tissue begins to regrow, you'll take oral medication. You'll only have to come to the clinic every few weeks for testing and possible further IV chemotherapy. The longer you remain in remission, the better your chances for a complete recovery."

"And if there is no complete recovery?" Melissa's mind was spinning, but the question popped out. Somehow, his words sounded ominous.

Dr. Rowan's expression grew somber, and he touched her arm; his eyes were filled with deep compassion. "I believe in being honest with my patients,

Melissa. I believe in being truthful because it's necessary for them to actively participate in the treatment of their disease. I'm not going to lie to you, but I won't leave you without hope either. People *do* survive leukemia. If you remain in a continuous first remission for five years, we consider you cured."

"And if I don't?"

"We try for a second remission. We also consider a bone marrow transplant. That's the grafting of healthy marrow from a biologically compatible donor into your marrow."

Suddenly, Melissa felt overwhelmed by too much information that threatened to split her head open. She couldn't stand to hear any more that Dr. Rowan had to say.

Mercifully, her mother interrupted. "What are you going to be doing for Melissa right now?"

"Today we'll do a lumbar puncture. We'll take fluid from around Melissa's spinal cord and examine it to determine if the leukemic cells have invaded your central nervous system. That test will also help us decide on the best combination of drugs to begin fighting your leukemia."

Melissa understood that suddenly her body had become a war zone. Her internal defenses no longer controlled what was happening inside of her. "When will you start the drugs?"

"Tomorrow."

"So soon?"

"Clinically, the disease progresses rapidly. We must begin treatment immediately." The pressure of his large, warm hand on her arm made her nod almost imperceptibly.

"Do it," she said, gazing toward her mother and Michael. "Hurry and get started. I want to go home."

* * *

Melissa lay curled in a fetal position on her hospital bed. She felt empty. How long had she cried? An hour? Two? After the lumbar procedure, she'd been returned to her room. Someone brought a supper tray, but it sat untouched on her bedstand.

"You should eat, Melissa. You have to keep your strength up." Her mother's voice caused her to stiffen.

"For what?" Melissa asked, her own voice quivering. "So they can bleed me again? Stick me with more needles?"

"I'm sorry, honey . . ."

"Sorry!" Melissa flopped over and glared straight at her mother's face. "Is that all you can say? That you're sorry?"

"What do you want me to say?"

Melissa ignored the pinched look around her mother's mouth and the strained expression in her eyes. She wanted someone to hurt as much as she was hurting. "It's probably *your* fault, you know. You had me! You must have caused it."

"That's not true! The doctor assured me that cancer is not necessarily inherited and it's not contagious. It's a disease that can strike anyone."

"Why did it have to happen to me?" The sobs started again, but when her mother reached over to comfort her, Melissa pushed her away. "Go away. Just go away and leave me alone."

"Melissa, please . . ."

Melissa refused to listen. All she wanted was to be left alone. She turned to face the blank wall, twisting the bed sheet into a ball under her chin. She wasn't sure when her mother left, but she sensed she was alone again. She'd hurt her mother. She knew that, but it was too late to change it now. *So what?* she thought. *Life is full of pain*.

"Hello, Melissa."

Ricter Davis. Why wouldn't everybody leave her alone? "Go away," she mumbled.

"It's Ric."

"I know who it is. I don't want to talk to anybody."

"Because you have cancer?"

The word seemed dirty, unclean. She rolled over to face him, enraged and ready to lash out at him. "What I have is none of your business."

Ric lifted himself onto her bed and laid the metal crutches across the end of her mattress. "Let's talk about it."

"I don't want to talk."

"Sometimes talking helps."

His eyes were empathetic, and for the first time Melissa's hostility wavered. "You knew what they were testing me for the other night. Why didn't you tell me?" Her words were accusing.

"Why didn't you ask?"

"I didn't *know* enough to ask."

"They do bone marrow studies to rule out leukemia. You should have asked your doctor if you were curious."

It was as if he'd told her it was her fault she hadn't been forewarned about her diagnosis. Her anger flared again. "Drop dead."

His smile was sardonic. "I might just do that."

"Meaning?"

"Meaning I know where you're at. I have cancer, too."

His revelation left her groping for words. "I . . . I didn't know . . ."

"It's not leukemia, like yours. It's osteogenic sar-

coma—bone cancer. That's why they cut off my leg."
He motioned to the void below his thigh. She shud-
dered in spite of herself. "Repulsive, isn't it? Not to
mention the crimp it's put in my track career."

"Track?"

"I was a marathoner for the University of South
Florida. Had a scholarship and everything." He
slapped the stump of his leg. "Not much of an Olym-
pic future for a one-legged runner."

"I'm sorry . . ."

"I went through the chemo part, too." His eyes
held hers without mercy, without pity. "It's no picnic,
but you *can* do it."

Melissa swallowed hard and wished she could escape her nightmare. *This can't be happening to me.
Not me.* She sat up and hugged her knees to her chest,
suddenly self-conscious that she wore nothing beneath
the thin cotton gown. "Why are you in the hospital
now?"

"More tests. Just to see if it's spread to other parts
of my body."

"And?"

"And so far, I'm clean."

"That's good, isn't it?"

"Real good." His voice had dropped so low, she
had to lean forward to catch it. "The physical therapist
is trying out a new prosthesis on me. That's an artificial
limb. The last one caused skin ulcers because it didn't
fit right."

Melissa shut her eyes and sighed. She didn't
want to be hearing about this. There was a horror in it
all that nauseated her. Ric was only a few years older
than she was—too young for cancer. She raked her
hand through her hair, shaking it out of her face. It
billowed, comfortingly, against her back. She re-

flected on an earlier part of their conversation. "The chemo," she asked. "What's it really like?"

His gaze went guarded. "It doesn't matter what it's like. It's something you have to do."

His evasive answer frightened her. "Tell me, Ric. Please."

"You'll be sick."

"I understand."

"No, you don't. You'll be so sick, you'll wish you could die."

Tears welled inside her but she fought them down. She refused to cry in front of him. "Does anything help?"

"Try to eat, even when you know it won't stay down. Don't be a stoic—get mad, cry if you want to. And don't go through it alone. If your family can't be with you when you're heaving up your guts, get a nurse."

Coldness crept up her spine and she sat motionless. The one small, weak light over her hospital bed could not dispel the gloom. She felt Ric shift off of her mattress.

"Where are you going?" Momentary panic set in as she realized she didn't want to be alone. Her feelings for Ric had done a 180-degree turn. Now she didn't want him to leave.

"Back to my room."

"Do you have to? I'm scared."

Unexpectedly, his hand reached out, caught her chin, and lifted it. His eyes locked onto hers. "Jesus, you're pretty."

There was a sadness in his whispered words she didn't understand. "So what? What do my looks have to do with anything?"

"Just an observation." Ric shrugged, but she felt

baffled, as if his remark had a deeper meaning she couldn't quite grasp. "Your doctors will send someone in to teach you about positive imaging, Melissa. It's sort of a mind-over-matter approach to healing. Listen to her and do exactly what she tells you. No matter how bad it gets, don't give up."

"Will you come back?"

A mysterious smile twisted the corner of his mouth. "Of course. We're alike, you know. Pretty soon you won't have a whole lot in common with your former world."

Images flashed through her mind: home, school, Jory, Brad. A gulf separated them from her and the sterile, bleak walls of the hospital. "I won't let that happen," she said.

"We'll see." At the doorway he paused and looked at her with a long, soul-searching stare. "Too bad about your hair."

"What about it?"

"The chemo will take it. It'll take it all."

Chapter Nine

"You heard me, Jory. Cut it." Melissa eyed the scissors in her friend's hand, ignoring Jory's startled look.

"When you asked me to sneak a pair of scissors up to your room, I didn't know you were planning on cutting off your hair. Come on, Melissa . . . What gives?"

Sitting cross-legged on her bed, Melissa pressed her lips together in steely determination. Her testing had been completed, and just an hour ago Dr. Rowan had informed her and her mother of the course of treatment he had prescribed for her case.

"I've written down the names of the drugs, their frequency of administration, and their side effects." He had given Melissa a piece of paper with neatly typed columns, but she had resisted reading it. "You'll be taking pills, getting injections, and taking some medications intravenously so we can regulate their entrance into your bloodstream more easily. Blood work will be done daily, bone marrow exams once every two weeks during induction. These drugs are very powerful, and by killing off the leukemic cells, they threaten the healthy ones, too."

"In short," Melissa had interrupted. "You're killing me softly with the medicine."

Dr. Rowan had crossed his arms over his broad, barrel-shaped chest. "We're saving you slowly from your disease," he had corrected. "You'll be given your first doses immediately, and you'll go down to the special chemo room in a little while."

Once he'd left, Melissa had taken her pills and endured a stinging shot that instantly nauseated her. She had urged her mother to go to work and stop back later in the afternoon, and then called Jory, catching her before she'd gone off to school. "Come by the hospital first," she had said. "And bring your scissors."

Now, as Jory clutched the scissors tightly, Melissa told her, "They'll be coming to take me down for my first round of chemo real soon. I want my hair cut before they walk in the door. Are you going to do it for me, or do I have to do it myself?"

"But, Melissa," Jory argued, "you've had long hair all your life. And it's so gorgeous. Why chop it off now? It doesn't make any sense."

"It's got to come off," Melissa said woodenly, fighting fiercely to hold back her tears. "I'd rather take it off myself than have the chemotherapy do it for me."

"I don't understand."

"Oh, Jory, stop acting so dumb! The chemo will make it all fall out. It's a side effect. It's the price I have to pay for a cure. Now do you get it?"

"I . . . I didn't realize . . . I'm sorry, Melissa. Really sorry."

"Yeah—well, so am I. But being sorry won't change it. By the time they finish giving me the drugs to make me well, I'll be bald. If I cut it now, myself, maybe that won't be so horrible."

Jory hesitated, studying the scissors. "I'm not a beautician, you know."

Melissa punched her friend's arm playfully. "I've seen you take scissors to your own hair plenty of times. Like in freshman year, when you were in your punk phase and you spiked your hair. . . . Remember?"

Jory cringed. "That was the only time my parents ever noticed me. My father yelled for a week. It reflected on his image at the country club to have such a spaced-out daughter, you know."

Melissa heard the bitterness in Jory's voice. She closed her hand around Jory's and whispered, "Let's get started, okay?"

Jory flashed an impish smile. "If this works out, maybe I'll move to Australia and take up sheep shearing." She combed the dark, thick hair, slipped the scissors into the shining mass next to Melissa's ear and cut.

In minutes, the bed was covered with hair. Melissa closed her eyes and sat perfectly straight, feeling her head grow lighter as the hair fell away. Cool air fanned the exposed nape of her neck and she shivered. The silence in the room was broken only by the steady snip of the metal blades. Even Jory, usually bubbling with chatter, was quiet.

"What the hell is going on!" The roar of Michael's voice made Melissa jump, and Jory squealed as the scissors clattered to the floor.

Michael grabbed Jory roughly by the shoulders, his face pinched and angry. "What are you doing to my sister?"

Jory gaped numbly, her eyes round and wide and her hands clenched behind her.

Melissa reached out and grasped Michael's arm. "Stop it, Michael! Let go of her. It's not her fault—I asked her to cut my hair."

"You what?" He turned his fury on her. "Why the hell did you do a stupid thing like that?"

Melissa squared her chin and mustered a steely

ook. "Because the chemotherapy will make me go bald, and I refuse to let it have my hair. *I'm* taking it off before the medicine does, and I asked Jory to help me. Now tell her you're sorry."

Jory had turned stiff and ghostly white, obviously shaken by Michael's outrage. Michael clenched his fists and worked his jaw, clearly trying to control his emotions. "I'm sorry, Jory." He faced his sister and lifted what was left of her newly cut hair off her forehead. "Are you sure about the chemo?"

"Dr. Rowan gave me a list of side effects to expect." She reached for the paper on her night table. "He was very honest. But then, he told us from the start that he would be. Let's hear it for honestly," she mumbled under her breath. "Anyway, he said that the chemo causes lots of problems. Losing my hair is only one. But he also said that once I'm in remission and I go on maintenance therapy, my hair will grow back."

Michael gently stroked her head.

"It's only *hair* Michael," she said through clenched teeth.

"That's true. And now that I see it short, I like it. Although the style leaves something to be desired."

His attempt at humor calmed her. "Jory insisted she wasn't a beautician, but I made her cut it anyway."

"It's not that bad," Jory said, stepping closer to the side of the bed. "I mean, with a little mousse, a little curl, it could be really chic."

Michael hugged Melissa and she squeezed her eyes shut. "I'm scared, Michael."

"Do you want me to stay with you for your treatment?"

She did and she didn't. "No. It's all right."

"I'll stay," Jory offered.

"You're already skipping school."

"So what? It's not like I've never done *that* before, you know."

"The nurses will be with me," Melissa hedged. She began to sense her illness and treatments as a wall rising between herself and the "well" world. She'd been thrown into a different place the others could not fully enter, and she might as well come to terms with that now. She recalled Ric's message from the night before: *You won't have a whole lot in common with your former world.* "You two leave and come back tonight. I'll probably have oodles to tell you by then," she said.

"If you're sure . . ." She saw a guilty look of relief in Michael's eyes. She knew that hospitals and needles scared him.

"Go on." He was almost to the door when she called him back. "I—uh—forgot to ask . . . How's Mom?"

"She's pretty rung out."

Guilt pricked at Melissa's conscience. "I said some things to her last night I didn't mean. I'm so sorry. You'll tell her I'm sorry, won't you?"

"You can tell her. She's planning on coming by during her lunch hour."

"I really am sorry, Michael."

He nodded, his blue eyes holding hers. "We're all sorry, Melissa. Everything about this business stinks. But we're family, and we'll make it through."

Once Michael left, Jory sighed. "Why do I always act like such a fool in front of him?"

Melissa picked up a lock of hair from the bed and it fell through her fingers. *Lucky Jory.* Nothing more heavy to think about than acting silly in front of a guy she wants to impress. She asked, "Could you help me clean this up before you go? I don't want them to bring me back to a hairy bed."

Neither of them spoke as they scooped up the wads of hair and threw them into the wastepaper basket. Together they brushed off the mattress until no wayward strands could be found on the clean white sheets. When they hugged each other goodbye, Melissa sensed a tension between them. Jory could walk out the door. Melissa could not. Jory had school and friends and everyday life to return to. Melissa had chemotherapy to face. She ran her fingers through her cropped hair and settled against her pillows to wait for the technicians.

The chemo room wasn't anything like Melissa expected. It was painted buttercup yellow, with bold graphic prints on the walls and gray carpeting. There were beige contour chairs that looked to be quite expensive. The only thing that belied the serene comfort of the room was the metal IV stand beside each chair.

"Hi, Melissa," a nurse said cheerfully. "I'm DeeDee Thomas, and I'll be administering your medication."

Feeling more terrified than sociable, Melissa forced herself to acknowledge the nurse's chatter while DeeDee inserted a needlelike contraption of plastic tubing and a rubber plug into a vein in her arm. "This is a heparin lock," DeeDee explained. "Not very glamorous-looking, but you'll wear it for the next few days. That way, we have access to your blood supply and can administer your chemo regime without having to jab you so often."

Melissa wondered if she was supposed to feel grateful. She lay back in the chair and DeeDee hung a bag of liquid on the IV stand next to her bed. "Relax," the nurse said. "This will take about an hour."

An hour! Melissa saw her days dripping away through snaking lines of flexible tubing. "I feel sick to my stomach," she said.

DeeDee patted her shoulder and handed her a small bowl. "In case you need to vomit," she told her. Her eyes were kind, but they didn't even attempt to hide the truth from Melissa.

"It's going to be bad, isn't it?"

"What seems bad now is ultimately for your good. I'll be here for you if you need me."

Melissa swallowed against her own bile and swore to hold back as long as she could. She watched the fluid trickle from the inverted bottle and down the tubing into her arm. She watched as it began its long, steady journey into the microscopic battleground in her body.

That evening Melissa was too sick to eat dinner, too sick to receive visitors. Her mother held her through it all, but Michael had to leave because he couldn't stand to see her hurting. After her mother left, Melissa fell into a fitful sleep, awakening when she had to vomit again.

In the stillness of her room she sensed someone next to her bed. A hand smoothed her bangs from her brow. "I'm here, Melissa," Ric said.

"Go away," she murmured through parched lips.

"It's worse to be alone," he whispered, blotting her cheek with a damp cloth.

She didn't want anyone to see her this way—exposed, vulnerable. Yet his hands were gentle and knowing. "You were right," she said when the violent nausea had subsided. "I do feel like I want to die."

"Haven't you heard?" he chided tenderly. "Only the good die young."

"I hate the way they treat me."

"Who?"

"The doctors. The people here."

"How do they treat you?"

"Like I'm not a person. Like I'm just a blob of cells. Like there's something unclean inside me and they've got to drive it out . . . no matter how much it hurts."

"Should I call up a witch doctor? Or a sorcerer?"

She managed to smile, despite her discomfort. "During treatment today, the psychologist came and taught me about 'imaging.'"

"So what will you use to hunt down and destroy your cancer cells? I pretend I'm manning a ship like Luke Skywalker. I close my eyes and zip through my body firing laser shots at any cancer cells trying to hide and multiply." He demonstrated by pointing his forefinger and making zinging sounds.

Melissa envisioned his illustration and smiled. "I imagine my cancer cells as hairy toads, all black and bony, with large suction cups for mouths. And they're sitting inside my bones sucking out my marrow, getting fat and strong while my marrow gets thinner and thinner."

Ric arched his eyebrow. "Grim picture. So what are you using to destroy them?"

"I . . . I haven't thought of something yet."

"That's the most important part, Melissa. That's what imaging is all about. You've got to see yourself hunting down the cells and destroying them. That's how you turn on your inner healing reserves."

Another wave of sickness churned through her and she clutched the sheets until her knuckles went white. "I . . . I can't think of anything stronger than those toads . . ." she said as her nausea turned into pain.

"You have to," Ric said, uncoiling her fingers from the sheet and making her grip his hand. "Don't you understand, Melissa? Your life depends on how hard you fight."

Chapter Ten

The chemical war intensified, and Melissa experienced battle fatigue. There were setbacks. A reaction to one of her medications that caused a horrible rash. A brief secondary infection that took an extra week to clear up. Melissa's stay in the hospital lengthened, and she felt more and more estranged from her former world.

Melissa knew she wasn't the only one having trouble coping. Her mother came daily with tense smiles and false bravado. Michael came, always nervous and fidgeting, revealing to Melissa that he'd rather be anywhere but at the hospital. Jory visited often, but Melissa adamantly refused to let any of her other friends come up to see her.

Late afternoon sun slanted through the blinds as Jory bounced into Melissa's room, talking nonstop. "Sorry I didn't get by last night. Steve and Melanie and Dirk and I went out for pizza, and Dirk was cash poor so I had to fork it over—boy, did that steam me. I mean, why pay for your own date?" Jory paused long enough to take a breath, and Melissa forced a smile.

Jory's visits were the hardest. She always had stories to tell of school and parties and dates. Melissa listened, hating to hear them, yet longing for them.

"I'm sure he'll pay you back, or at least treat you next time."

"He'd better." She tossed her books on the floor along with a sack. "Listen to me, going on and on. How're things going for you today?"

"Except for chemo, my schedule's open."

"This must be such a drag for you."

"The high point of my day is when they come to disinfect the bathroom," Melissa said.

"How is the food? You really should eat more. You look thinner."

"I know. I've lost twelve pounds in eight days."

Jory grimaced. "Can't keep anything down, huh?"

"I didn't think it was possible to throw up so much."

"And me rattling on about pizza. Sorry about that."

"Let me make my pity party complete," Melissa said, tugging gently on her hair. A handful fell weightlessly to the floor. "How can you stand to look at me?" she asked, touching the sores that erupted on her face.

Jory's green eyes grew wide. "You're not that ugly. I . . . I mean . . ."

Melissa released a short, bitter laugh. "Real homecoming queen material, huh? And how about the junior prom? Who'll want to ask the Bride of Frankenstein?"

Jory picked up the paper bag that lay with her books. "Here. This is for you."

"What is it?"

"Scarves. I bought them in that boutique we used to shop at in the mall."

Melissa momentarily forgot her misery as she fingered the selection of colorful, filmy scarves. "Silk, Jory?" she asked, lifting her hairless eyebrow. She knew that each elegant piece of cloth must have cost double digits. The irony was not lost on her. Jory never had to give a second thought to what things cost. Or who would ask her for a date. She didn't have to struggle with anything more incapacitating than a hangnail. "Thank you, Jory. It was nice of you."

"Do you like them? I picked out what I thought you'd like best. They are okay, aren't they?"

Her eagerness to please touched Melissa deeply. "They're great." Melissa tied a paisley scarf around her balding head.

"Good grief, you look like a bag lady. Here . . . let me do it." Melissa reached for a surgical mask and covered her mouth and nose.

"Why'd you do that?" Jory asked.

Melissa felt overwhelmed suddenly. How could she explain to Jory that the disease was *hers* and she had to join the doctors in the fight against it? Melissa knew that being careful and taking precautions from now on meant helping with her cure.

"Dr. Rowan says I have to be careful not to catch anything. Even a cold could set me back weeks."

"What do I look like? A germ bank?"

"It's nothing personal, really. I just want to get out of here so bad . . ."

Jory slouched in a chair on the far side of the room. Melissa hadn't meant to hurt her feelings and didn't know how to make it up to her.

"So tell me more about school," Melissa said brightly. "Does anyone ask about me?"

"Sure. As a matter of fact, Brad asked me about you today."

Melissa's heart leaped in spite of herself. The afternoon she'd spent with Brad at the country club seemed like a million years ago. And although she didn't want anyone but Jory visiting her, she wouldn't mind if he called. But he hadn't. Not once. "How's Brain Bowl coming? Are they still holding my place open on the team?"

"You mean you still want to do Brain Bowl?"

Jory's surprise irked her. "Of course. Once this part of my treatment is over and I start looking human again, I *will* come back to school."

Jory flushed and stared into her lap. "I—uh— well Brad did say that they were talking about replacing you . . ."

"Don't let them do it, Jory." Melissa grew agitated, twisting the bed sheet into a ball.

"But Melissa, you're so sick. Why does it matter to you now?"

"Because it just does." Her voice went thick with emotion. "Because it's mine. That seat on the Brain Bowl team belongs to *me*."

"Do you want me to ask Mr. Marshall or Mrs. Watson about it?"

"Would you?"

"Well, they've certainly talked with me on enough occasions," Jory observed dryly. "In fact, if you remember, Watson threatened to flunk me last year. I guess I could chat with her on your behalf."

Melissa felt relieved, but the intense emotions had drained her energy and she eased down against her pillow. "I'd really appreciate it, Jory. I mean, I could ask my mom, but I don't think she could handle one more thing. My leukemia is wringing her out."

"How's Michael taking it?"

"He avoids it. I don't think he means to. No one really wants to talk about it with me except the medical types."

Jory picked at the blue polish on her fingernails. "So who do you talk with here?"

"Ric. Sometimes."

"That's the guy with—" Jory paused, "—with the bone cancer."

"The guy with one leg, you mean," Melissa said, knowing Jory was embarrassed. "Don't worry, it took me a while to get used to being honest about it, too. At least once I'm in remission, I'll look normal again. That's what they tell me anyhow. Ricter Davis never will."

"When do you think you'll get out of here? Have they said?"

"My blood work's looking better. My platelet count has stabilized and my white blood count has fallen. My doctors say it's a good sign, but they also say that I still have a long way to go. Once I'm discharged, I have to go on outpatient therapy."

"What's outpatient?"

"I can go home, but I have to come here for chemo and bone marrow exams and blood tests until I achieve remission."

"How long will that take?"

Melissa shrugged her thin shoulders. "They don't know. But once I do go into remission, I'll still have to take some of the drugs for a long time. Maybe years. And I'll have to keep coming to the clinic for testing."

"But you'll be all right?" Jory picked the words carefully. "You'll be well again?"

"I don't know what 'all right' means anymore. I'll still have leukemia. But the longer I stay in remission, the better my chances of being cured. Five years without a recurrence and I'm home free." The smile Melissa offered felt stiff and forced.

"And if you don't stay in remission?"

Melissa studied her friend. She'd turned the statistics and facts over and over in her head for days, ever since she'd asked Dr. Rowan the very same thing. Suddenly she wanted to talk about it, get it into the open and out of the dark corners of her mind. "They're going to do a bone marrow aspiration on Michael next week," she confided.

"Is Michael sick, too?" A look of fear crossed Jory's face and she bolted upright in the chair.

"No. It's for me. To see if his bone marrow is compatible with mine in case I ever need a transplant. They harvest a bunch of his marrow and put it into my bones and wait to see if it will grow and take over for my own." *A bunch*. Is that how bone marrow grows? In an unscientific bunch? Like a cluster of flowers? She cleared her throat. "If it does, no more leukemia. But Dr. Rowan says it's risky. And I could reject the transplant."

Jory's round, green eyes widened and Melissa prayed that Jory wouldn't pursue the next most logical question: *What if you reject the transplant?* "I hope they can fix it the other way. With the chemo and all," Jory finally said.

"Me too."

Jory stood, fidgeting with the strap on her purse. "Well I guess I should be going. I've got a geometry test tomorrow."

Melissa felt childish longing. "I wish I did."

"Are you able to do much studying? I've brought all your textbooks. But maybe you need something special from the library. I'll bring anything you want."

"I'm keeping up. Mom got each of my teachers to outline assignments for me. When I go back to school, I can take a few tests to see if I'm up to par with the

est of the class. It's important that I keep up, you
now." She focused her attention on a blank spot on
he wall behind Jory.

Jory shifted from one foot to the other. "The
SATs are scheduled for the third Saturday in Oc-
ober."

Melissa's vision zeroed in on her friend. *The
SATs!* How could she have forgotten them? Es-
ecially when she pinned her hopes on scoring high
nough to qualify as a National Merit Scholar. "In the
.incoln auditorium?" she asked.

"Yes, starting at eight-thirty A.M. sharp. Bring
wo number-two lead pencils. Don't fold, spindle, or
nutilate your IBM punch card."

Melissa sighed. "I've got to get out of this place."

"The test's less than two weeks away."

"I don't care. I'm going to take it."

"They'll have a makeup test."

"No. I'm going to take it with my class."

"Oh, Melissa, do you think you should plan on
hat?" Jory asked.

"Why not? If I'm an outpatient, like they said I'll
e, there's no reason why I can't go."

"But you've been so sick . . ."

"So I'll bring a barf bag." Defiance and anger
verwhelmed her. "I'm sick and tired of people telling
ne what I can and can't do. Don't I get to make any
hoices for my life?" By now her hands were shaking
nd she tasted tears in the back of her throat.

"I was just worried, that's all," Jory said.

"Well, stop worrying. I'm going to survive this.
'm not going to fade away like a shadow. I'm *alive*,
lamn it!"

"I know you are." Jory's voice held a note of hys-
eria. "It's just all so horrible, that's all. I hate it."

"And I don't?" The burst of anger had sapped he
She shut her eyes as the room spun and nausea ove
came her. Fine beads of perspiration broke out on he
forehead as she fought against the sickness, but sh
knew she was losing the battle and said, "Jory, th
basin . . ."

Jory clamored across the room and got the basi
to her just in time. Melissa heaved until there wa
nothing left. Jory had dampened a washcloth an
wiped her face for her. "Should I ring for a nurse?" sh
asked.

"No. It's over." Melissa lay back on the bed. Sh
heard Jory moving around the room—flushing th
toilet, running water, and returning the basin to he
bedside table. When she had the strength to ope
her eyes, she saw Jory standing next to her, staring a
her thoughtfully. "Some friend I am. I throw up a
over you." She was too weak to even feel embarrassed

"I'm glad I was here and that you weren't alone.
Jory kept studying Melissa's face, as if seeing her fo
the first time. Melissa wished she didn't look so horri
ble.

"Hey, your scarf's twisted," Jory said.

"Will you fix it?" The ulcers in her mouth burne
and it was difficult to speak.

Jory eased the surgical mask over Melissa's face
"No use taking any chances on your catching anything
Especially now that you're so close to getting out c
this dump." She retied the scarf in a jaunty fashion
with the knot to one side.

"You're a good friend," Melissa said.

Jory's voice turned crisp and businesslike. "An
don't worry about Brain Bowl. I'll talk to the power
that be. They won't dare drop you from the team."

"How can you guarantee that?" Melissa was struggling to form words and stay awake.

"Blackmail. How could they even consider dropping a poor, sick girl who's just counting the days till she's able to compete with her team?"

Melissa smiled. "You're devious, Jory Delaney."

"Yeah. I know." Jory wiped her friend's forehead one more time. "And we'll go take the PSATs together. I'll even hold your barf bag if you want."

"I might have to bring a bag to wear over my head, too. Don't want to frighten all my classmates, do I?"

"Who cares? All that matters is that you ace the test for that scholarship."

"You could ace it, too . . ." Her voice was barely a whisper.

"College isn't for me, Melissa. Unless you count the frat parties. Now go to sleep, and I'll be back tomorrow after school." Melissa's eyes were already closed and Jory's voice sounded far away.

When she woke up, the twilight had cast long violet shadows across her room. Ric was holding her hand. "Hey, lady," he said, a half-smile lighting his gaunt features.

"Hey."

Without asking, Ric placed a mint on her tongue. "Rough day?"

"Real rough." Melissa noticed that he was dressed in street clothes, jeans and a polo shirt. "Got a date?"

He placed the back of her hand along the length of his cheek. His skin felt cool and slightly rough. "I've been discharged, Melissa. I'm going home."

Chapter Eleven

Melissa filled with envy. *Home.* When would she be able to say the same thing? "I'm happy for you, Ric. Where's home?"

"Upstate New York. But I'm really only returning to my dorm room at USF. After two years of living there, I think of it as home."

"So you'll be here at the university?" In a strange way she was relieved. He was the only person she knew close to her own age who understood what it was like to have cancer.

"At least until the end of the spring term. Then I'll probably stay around for the summer and work until the fall semester starts."

"Don't you want to go back to New York for the summer? And see your family?"

His gaze was direct, and she noticed how dark and piercing his eyes were. "My medical support is here in Tampa. I don't want to leave."

The notion stunned her. *Her* medical support was here too. How would that affect her choice of colleges? Melissa kept her concerns to herself, offering Ric a half-smile. "When you're dressed in jeans, you can't even tell about your leg."

His expression was cynical. "Yeah, this prosthesis is terrific. No one could even guess I'm a cripple unless I break into a run."

"Ric, it doesn't make you less of a person."

"Just three-fourths of one."

"But there're no more signs of your cancer."

He flipped the ends of her scarf. "That doesn't mean it won't come back. There are no guarantees."

Her stomach lurched, but not from chemo. His blunt pessimism made her feel as if she were trapped in a labyrinth of blind alleys and stone walls. "Where's that optimistic guy who sat by my bed while I tossed my cookies every night?"

Ric took her hand. "He's still inside me, Melissa." His scrutiny made her feel uneasy because she knew how horrible she looked, broken out in sores and skin lesions from the medications. "I'm going to call you when you're back home. After the worst is over and you're back in classes."

"Why?" Her heart thudded crazily, but not the way it had when Brad had touched her. She wasn't sure how to sort out the differences between Brad's and Ric's touches and the way they made her feel. And she didn't know why; although she was attracted to both of them, it seemed to be in different ways.

"Because I want to," Ric said. "Because, like I told you before, we're alike."

"Just because we both have cancer doesn't mean we're alike." She wasn't sure why his comparison put her off.

He grinned beguilingly. "All right, then, because I think you're one foxy lady and I want to date you."

Surprised by his confession, she said, "I look totally gross, and you know it."

"But you won't always look 'totally gross.' Once they get you into remission, you'll look just like you did before. Very pretty."

Her hand automatically touched her head.

"Except for my hair. I'll never be able to grow it tha long again." Secretly she still mourned for it, but she didn't regret having cut it. At least *that* decision had been hers and hers alone.

Ric's eyes grew somber and he stared long and deep into hers. "Take care, Melissa. I'll be calling you You can count on it."

She watched him leave, feeling a strange mix o emotions. Part of her felt dependent upon him. Part o her felt freed from having him checking on her, identi fying with her, as if he knew what was inside her mind and soul when she grappled with having cancer. The truth was, she wasn't dealing with it. "It," the cancer was an alien creature that had invaded her body and was gorging itself on her good health.

The doctors, the psychiatrists, the lab techni cians—they were foreigners, too. She knew they were trying to help her, but they also seemed like invaders. They had assaulted her dignity—uncovering, poking, revealing, peeling layers of shyness away from her body like dead skin, removing it, strip by strip, until she felt naked and personless. She was still thinking and struggling with her problem when the nurse came to take her down for another round of chemo.

The next morning Michael came to see her. Al though she hated for him to see her when she wasn't on top of her nausea, his presence always comforted her. "I'm between work and class," he said, his eyes darting uneasily around her room. "I don't have too much time."

"I'm glad you came anyway. This place is the pits and I want out." He placed the surgical mask over her mouth for her and sat next to her bed, leaning on the mattress and resting his chin on his fist. He reminded her of a forlorn puppy. "When was the last time you went ballooning?"

"I don't remember."

"You need to go soon. You look earthbound."

A smile started at the corners of his mouth. "Will you go with me when you get home?"

"Haven't I thrown up enough lately? You know how I react to heights."

"Then will you drive the chase car like before?"

"Can I bring Jory?"

He made a face. "You still trying to fix me up with her?"

"Who else is there in your life?"

He touched her cheek. "Only you, Sis."

"Are you bothered about them doing the bone marrow test on you, Michael?" She'd wanted to ask him for days, but hadn't found the right moment. "I know how you hate needles."

"It's for *you*. Let them stick me." He sounded braver than he looked about it.

"Maybe we won't be compatible."

"Then they'll find a donor who is."

The idea frightened her. Somehow the transplant seemed less intimidating if it came from her brother. The thought of having some nameless, faceless stranger living inside her bones made her shudder.

"But we will be compatible," Michael said, trying to comfort her. "And besides, this chemo stuff is going to work, so you won't even need a transplant. You shouldn't even be thinking about it."

"I hope it works. I'd hate to think I was this miserable for nothing." He grinned at her sullen humor. "How's Mom doing?" Melissa asked. "She acts cheerful enough when she visits me, but how's she really doing?"

"Better. Once you two made up and she stopped feeling responsible . . ."

"Oh, that was my fault. She shouldn't feel responsible. Cancer isn't genetic. That was just a cheap shot I took because I was so angry about all of this."

"I think she felt that she should have noticed something was going on with you. That you weren't well. I guess I should have been more observant too."

Melissa was surprised. It hadn't occurred to her that her family might feel guilty about her illness. "It wasn't anybody's fault," she said.

Michael shrugged as if he didn't quite believe her. "Mom's raided the library and the medical textbook section at the bookstores for every printed word about leukemia. You should see her tackle your doctor—she bombards him with a million questions. He must hate to see her coming!"

Melissa pictured her mother giving Dr. Rowan the third degree. It dawned on her that her mother knew more about her disease than she did, and she was moved that her mother had gone to such lengths to read and ask questions about her treatments. "Maybe I'll read some of her books," she said. Although she was inspired by her mother, she wasn't sure how much more she wanted to know.

"I brought you a present," Michael said.

"You did? But you've already given me three stuffed animals and a vase of flowers. You should be saving your money for ballooning." The cuddly toys had been relegated to the windowsill so she could see them from her bed. Dr. Rowan didn't want them too near in case they harbored any microscopic germs.

She thought it was ridiculous. The animals looked only soft and friendly and innocent.

Michael reached for a bag he'd slipped beneath her bed and removed a book with a handsome cloth-and-leather cover. It smelled faintly of disinfectant, and as she thumbed through the pages she was moved by his attempt to "de-germ" it for her safety.

"All the pages are blank," she said.

"That's because it's a personal journal. You're supposed to write on the pages."

"Like a diary?"

"Kind of. You just write in it when you feel like it. You don't have to write every day if you don't want to."

She ran her palm over the supple, dark blue cover. "It's beautiful, Michael. Thanks. Dr. Moffat—that's the shrink who helps us deal with our cancer—" she rolled her eyes in exaggerated tolerance, "Dr. Moffat says writing down your feelings in letters or diaries is a good idea. She says it's therapeutic, but, I don't know . . . I think it sounds dumb."

"'Therapeutic'?" Michael grimaced good-naturedly. "If you're going to talk ugly, I'm taking my gift back. I just wanted to give you something to keep you busy." He paused, then said, "But maybe the shrink is right. Maybe you need to write about this whole stinking experience. In this book you can tell it like it is. And who knows—years from now, when you're rich and famous, you could have it published and make another million on your memoirs."

She smoothed her palm over the ivory-colored pages. "I'd rather think of it as portable bathroom walls where I can write all kinds of dirty words about these last few weeks."

Playfully, he grabbed at the book. "I didn't mean to create a monster."

"Don't touch my book." She held it against her breast and gave him a menacing glare. "Or I'll be sure and write unsavory things about you in it."

He laughed and stood. "Well, I've got to go. Mom's coming up during her lunch hour and that's not too long from now."

Melissa pulled the mask away from her mouth, allowing him to watch her lips as she said, "Promise me you'll take up your balloon some morning this week."

"I'll try."

"Did I tell you that I'm using your balloon in my imaging therapy?"

"You know you didn't." He leaned against the near wall, his thumbs hooked through the front belt loops of his jeans. "So tell me."

"Well, supposedly it's important for me to use my alpha brain cells to fight my leukemia. Some sort of holistic approach to cancer treatment." She shrugged her bony shoulders.

"It seems like a lot of mumbo jumbo, but I think I read something about that in Mom's books. So how does my balloon fit it?"

Enthused, she hunched forward. "I close my eyes and imagine that I'm riding in your balloon—without getting sick," she qualified. "I'm riding along through my bones, and whenever I see one of my cancer cells, I toss a firebomb at it. It blows up"—she snapped her fingers—"without ever touching me, because the balloon's basket protects me."

"Does it help?"

She heard the skepticism in his tone and said, "Yes, it does. After a really good session, after totally relaxing, I feel better. It helps me not to be so sick to my stomach after the chemo treatments, too."

"Whatever works."

"It does work, Michael. I know it sounds crazy, but it *does* work." She picked at her bed sheet. "I want to go home. I want everything to be normal again. I'll do whatever they want me to do in order to get out of here."

She watched him work his jaw. "It won't be much longer. You're bound to respond to all these treatments soon."

"That's what they keep telling me," she said. "So . . . how's my room at home? Does it miss me?"

His smile was brief and rather sad. "It misses you like crazy." She felt an overwhelming wave of homesickness wash over her.

"You'd better go before I try to crawl into your pocket and leave with you."

After he'd gone, Melissa tried doing a school assignment, but her attention wandered. She thought about so many things—home, the PSATs, Brain Bowl, her illness. Even if she did go home soon, how would she adjust? How could she ever think of herself as "normal" again?

She picked up the book Michael had given her and considered what to write in it. Should she describe what it felt like to stare mortality in the face? Or should she write about more practical things, like fighting to maintain her place on the Brain Bowl team? Or about trying to obtain a National Merit Scholarship that she might never use?

Or maybe she should explore her feelings about her family and friends. About how much she cared about them, and how precious they'd become during her illness. And what about life once she got out of the hospital? Who would ask her for a date? Who would ever kiss her or want her? Melissa sighed and thumbed through the blank pages. *Sixteen is too young to die*, she thought. She tossed the book aside, knowing that she had a lot to say and no earthly idea of how to say it.

Chapter Twelve

That afternoon, feeling stronger, Melissa asked a nurse to help her to the sun room. Located in the oncology ward, the room was lined with windows so that the sun streamed in and reflected off the antiseptically clean linoleum floors. Settling into a green upholstered chair, Melissa opened her history book and was soon lost in the drama of the Civil War.

"Hi. What'chya doing?"

Melissa jumped in her seat. A small girl was standing in front of her, holding a coloring book and a box of crayons tightly against her chest. "I'm reading," Melissa answered.

"What'chya reading?" The child was dressed in hospital pajamas a size too large for her tiny body. She had a fuzzy scramble of strawberry curls and big, bright blue eyes.

"I'm reading for school. It's homework."

"I'm going to kindergarten soon. Then I can read and do homework. My name's Rachael and I'm this many years old." She held up four fingers. A heparin lock was taped to her arm.

Melissa ignored the paraphernalia and concentrated on the child's upturned face. "I'm Melissa and I'm this many years old." She displayed ten fingers, then five and one.

Rachael studied them carefully. "Wow. You're old."

Melissa laughed. "You're right."

"I have leukemia," Rachael announced, dropping to her knees and opening her coloring book on the table next to Melissa's chair. "What have you got?"

Perhaps it was the child's unabashed honesty, her uncomprehending acknowledgment of their unlikely sisterhood, that brought a lump to Melissa's throat. "I have leukemia, too."

"I was in mission but now I'm not anymore."

A shudder ran up Melissa's spine. "You mean 'remission,' don't you?"

"Yup. I don't like it here, but Mommy says I have to stay for a while." Rachael flipped open the crayon box and dumped a rainbow of colored sticks across the table. The warm sunlight softened them, and the room became scented with the familiar smell of crayon wax.

"I don't like it here either, Rachael." Despite the sun, Melissa felt chilled. *A relapse*, she thought. Rachael had survived chemo, lived outside the hospital, then relapsed. Her leukemia had returned.

"I have a baby sister. Do you?"

"I have an older brother," Melissa said.

"Older?" Rachael glanced up from her coloring, her expression registering disbelief. "Are you friends?"

"Yes. Best friends."

"I don't like my sister very much. She cries a lot and keeps my mommy busy."

"You'll like her someday."

"Maybe." Rachael continued coloring and said, "The medicine they gave me makes me throw up."

Her sudden change of topics momentarily confused Melissa. "The medicine makes me throw up, too," she said.

"They stick needles in my back. Do they do that to you, too?"

"Yes."

"I used to think if they stuck me with needles everything inside would leak out. But that was when I was only three and I was still a baby."

Melissa bit her lower lip hard. She reached out and touched the soft, shining curls on Rachael's head. "Your hair's very pretty."

"It all fell out once. But now it's back." She beamed a broad smile. "Are you a mommy?"

The question struck Melissa like a splash of ice-cold water. Confused by a rush of emotions, she fumbled with her history book. The bright, sun-washed room was suddenly making her dizzy. "I have to go back to my room now, Rachael."

"Are you sick? Are you gonna throw up? I brought my dish just in case. Want to use it?" She held up the receptacle Melissa knew so well.

"No, thanks . . . It's just that I—I'm cold."

The child nodded. "Oh, I get cold at night. Sometimes when my mommy can't stay with me, I make the nurse bring me two blankets. She holds my hand till I go to sleep."

As Melissa slowly moved out the door she heard Rachael say, "Come visit me tomorrow, Melissa. Can we be friends?"

Safely back in her room, Melissa crawled between the sheets, her teeth chattering. She felt an overwhelming urge to cry but couldn't. *What's wrong with me? Why am I feeling this way?* She turned on her side and shivered. She squeezed her eyes shut, but she kept seeing Rachael's face.

When she opened her eyes, the first thing she spied on the bedside table was the journal. She reached for it, opening to the first cream-colored, fresh-smelling blank page. She sat up and rummaged in the metal drawer until she found a black felt-tip pen, and began writing in her most graceful penmanship.

> *I met a little girl today named Rachael. She's four and she has cancer, too. She thought I was very old, being sixteen, and I thought she was very sweet and too young for these things they're putting us through at the hospital. She asked me if I was a mommy. Of course, I'm not. But I can't help wondering if I ever will be. Who will want to make love to me now that I'm sick? What would it be like to have a baby grow inside of me? Will I ever know?*

Melissa reread the entry, underscored the last sentence, then put the journal away.

"Good morning, Melissa." Dr. Rowan breezed into her room the next day, his face lit with a smile, a clipboard and a manila folder in his hand.

Warily she lowered the textbook she was studying. "My lab results?"

"Your lab results." He flipped open the folder. "Your platelet count has stabilized and your white count is acceptable. However, there's a marked decrease of polys, which means you're still quite vulnerable to infection, so you'll have to avoid crowds and keep that surgical mask on when you go outside . . ."

"Outside?"

"I'm discharging you. Although we haven't achieved remission yet, I think we're close."

Her mouth went dry over the news. *I should be happy about this*, she thought. But in reality, she was scared. She hated the hospital, but there she was sheltered, and her doctors and nurses were at hand to help her. At home, she'd be on her own. "Is it really safe for me to leave?"

"It's both safe and necessary," Dr. Rowan said, shaking his head of unruly hair. "You need to start leading a normal life again. Get back into the mainstream."

Wasn't that what she wanted too? "But what if I have a problem?"

"Your family will be instructed how to deal with most things. And if there's something they can't handle, or if there are any questions, I'm a phone call away. You aren't being released from therapy, Melissa. Outpatient care is just one small step on the road to recovery."

"Can I go back to school?"

"Not right away."

"When?"

"I can't say yet. Your chemo program will change, but until you're on maintenance, I'd rather not have you in a classroom environment."

"I want to be back in school in another week."

"That's too soon, Melissa."

"When?"

"If all goes well, maybe after Christmas. It'll be safer then."

"Christmas! The school year will be half over by then."

"But you'll be stronger and more able to fight off infections."

Melissa struggled against panic. Dr. Rowan couldn't make her wait so long to return to school.

She'd already missed most of October and part of November. She couldn't stand the thought of staying out until January. "But the PSATs are being given next Saturday. I have to take them with my class. They're for college."

"You're a stubborn girl, Melissa. Of course, I can't forbid you, but it isn't a good idea."

Her palms were clammy. "It's one test for just a few hours. My friend Jory can take me, stay with me, bring me straight back home." She squared her chin. "I'll wear my mask the whole time." She imagined herself sitting in the vast auditorium with a surgical mask strapped to her face. The image caused her to shudder, but she'd do it if it meant she could take the test.

Dr. Rowan was speaking to her, but she heard only part of his speech. ". . . your mother comes I'll have your discharge papers ready. Someone can bring you to the clinic day after tomorrow for your chemo. DeeDee Thomas will administer it, so you'll still be seeing plenty of familiar faces. Feel free to come up here to the floor whenever you want to visit. It encourages the other patients, you know, seeing someone living on the outside. There's a teen support group that meets once a month which you might like to join."

Melissa nodded, unable to sort through all he was telling her. The only thing she cared about was that she was going home. When Jory called and Melissa told her, her friend squealed so loud Melissa had to hold the phone away from her ear.

"Everyone will be *so* glad!"

Melissa wanted everybody to know, but she didn't want anybody to visit her. She knew how bad she looked. "I can't have visitors," she added hastily.

"Oh sure. I understand that. But still, you'll be

home. It can't be too long before you can come back to school."

"Probably not," she lied. "About Brain Bowl . . ."

"No sweat," Jory assured. "Watson was the picture of sympathy and understanding. She said you made the final ten fair and square, and even though you haven't been drilling with them, she's sure you'll be up to speed in no time once you return."

Melissa sagged with relief, twisted the phone cord around her forefinger, and said, "I'm on for the PSATs, too. Dr. Rowan wasn't thrilled about my taking them, but I'm doing it anyway."

"Can I come to the hospital and help you pack up?"

"You don't have to. Mom will be here. Michael, too."

Melissa sensed the disappointment in a long pause and said, "What the heck. The more the merrier. Come on down."

After lunch Melissa changed into street clothes, the first she'd worn since her admission. Her jeans hung sadly on her thin body and she could almost count her ribs through her T-shirt. She didn't care. She was going home. She packed everything in paper bags and a suitcase except for one cuddly teddy bear. She gave it to a nurse at the central nurse's station. "This is for Rachael—the little four-year-old girl with the curly, reddish hair."

The nurse smiled. "Oh, you mean Rachael Dove. How nice of you, Melissa. She's down in chemo right now and this will be a special treat for her when they bring her back up. She's usually pretty sick after her treatments."

Melissa returned to her room and waited silently with Jory while her mother handled the paperwork and Michael lugged her things down in the elevator. The Pink Lady, a hospital volunteer, made her ride down in a wheelchair, and Melissa felt self-conscious rolling through the lobby. Once outside, she saw both her mom's and Jory's cars parked beside the curb. "Which chariot will it be?" Her mother asked.

"Do you mind if Jory takes me?"

Her mother's expression said that she did mind, but she said, "Of course not. I'll see you back at the house."

Hastily, Melissa asked, "You are riding with us, aren't you Michael?"

His blue eyes flashed her a knowing, tolerant look. "Sure."

"Would you—uh—like to drive?" Jory asked, offering him the keys.

Michael took them. "Why not."

"I'll sit in the back," Melissa said. "There's more room." Michael settled her in the backseat. The car felt familiar and comfortable and smelled faintly of Jory's jasmine perfume. "Can you put the top down?" Melissa asked.

Jory and Michael exchanged glances. "Is that a good idea?" Michael asked.

"I've been cooped up inside for two weeks. I want to feel the sun . . . smell fresh air. Please?"

When Michael lowered the top Melissa turned her face up to soak in the warmth of the sun. She breathed deeply the cool, dry autumn air until her head grew light and her body finally relaxed. "Home, James," she directed with a snap of her fingers.

Michael drove slowly, cautiously, stopping at yellow traffic lights instead of barreling through as he normally might do. Jory sat sideways in her seat, gazing at Michael contentedly. Melissa watched the sunlight play off her friend's hair and the breeze ruffle through Michael's. "We can go a little faster, you know," she said.

"No we can't," Jory replied. She reached into her glove compartment and removed a yellow diamond-shaped sign with black lettering. She stuck it to the windshield, beneath the rearview mirror. Melissa smiled when she read it: "Slow. Precious Cargo on Board."

Chapter Thirteen

"Do you like what we've done to your bedroom, honey?" Mrs. Austin's question made Melissa pause as she walked around her room.

"It's nice, Mom. Really. I had no idea . . ."

"Michael and I wanted to surprise you. He painted the walls and the woodwork, and I picked out the comforter and curtains."

Melissa fingered the powder-blue spread decorated with printed apricot-and-white long-stemmed lilies. The faint aroma of fresh paint hung in the air. "I mean it, Mom. It's beautiful. Thank you."

"Michael installed the phone, too." Melissa noticed the pale blue stylized headset on the night stand next to her bed. "It's one of those programmable kinds," Mrs. Austin continued eagerly. "He's already put numbers into the memory for my office, Dr. Rowan, the clinic and Jory. All you have to do is punch the memory key and the single digit of whoever you want, and it dials those numbers automatically. Nice, huh?"

"Very nice." Melissa picked up the receiver and studied it. The truth was that she'd be home alone most of the coming days and she needed the phone in case an emergency arose. Forcing away her fear, she recradled the receiver. "I really appreciate all you and Michael have done, Mom."

Mrs. Austin advanced and hugged her. "I'm so glad you're home, baby."

Her mother's sweet gardenia scent filled Melissa's senses as she cuddled snugly in her arms. "I'm going to be all right, Mom. I know I'm going to get well."

Mrs. Austin smoothed Melissa's patchy head of hair. "I know you are, too. Now, why don't you climb between those nice new sheets and let me bring you some vegetable soup."

"Homemade?"

"Just for you."

"I'd like that." Her mother's special soup had sustained her through everything from flu to chicken pox to bad days of menstrual cramps.

After Melissa had settled into bed, Michael came in. "It's really good to have you home," he said, sitting on the edge of the mattress.

"Thanks for painting my room. I like the color. Ivory makes the room look bigger. How come there's no programmed number for you on the phone?"

He shrugged. "Between school and two jobs, I doubted you could track me down. But I'll be home whenever I can."

"Still baby-sitting your kid sister, huh?"

He touched her chin. "Yep. And I'll even leave the baseball bat by your bed."

"Mom says you put Jory's number into the phone. How did you know it?"

"Stop baiting me. I looked it up in the phone book."

Melissa frowned. "You've got to admit, she's been a terrific friend. Oh, she was put off at first, but once she got used to my being sick, she came to see me a lot. She bought me all those scarves. She kept me entertained with stories of her social life and everything that's been going on at school, and she made sure I wasn't kicked off the Brain Bowl team."

"I like her car," Michael said dryly.

"Why are you so stubborn?"

"I like to see the fire in your eyes and the smoke curling out your ears."

"You're going to appreciate Jory someday, Michael. And I hope she won't give you the time of day when you're just aching to be with her either."

"The time off her Rolex watch?"

His grin was devilish, and Melissa felt her anger rising. "Out of my room!" She pointed toward the door.

He rose, laughing, and warded off the pillow she tossed at him. "It's good to have you home. Even if it does mean more visits from Jory Delaney."

"Out!"

"I love you, too," he called as he shut the door behind him.

In spite of her exasperation, Melissa smiled and slipped downward into the cozy comfort of her bed. Her eyes caressed her room. *Home*. She'd finally come home. Now all she had to do was go into remission and get well. Then maybe she could put this entire nightmare behind her and get on with the rest of her life.

"Don't you think we should go inside now?" Jory nervously tapped on the handle inside her car door.

"Just a few more minutes," Melissa told her, glancing first at her watch, then out the car window to see two more students straggle into the Lincoln High auditorium in the Saturday morning gloom. The day had arrived cool and gray.

"They lock the doors at eighty-thirty sharp," Jory said, chewing on her bottom lip.

"I know, Jory. Calm down. I'm not going inside until the last possible minute. Are you sure Mrs. Watson's saving special seats for us in the back row?"

"It's all arranged. We slip into the seats right before the test starts, and as soon as it's over, we get first dibs on slipping out."

Melissa took a deep breath, adjusted her scarf and wide-brimmed hat, and said, "Okay, let's go."

Jory buttoned her denim jacket against a blast of cool wind and stepped aside for Melissa to climb out of the car. "Do you have your"—she stopped—"you know. Your stuff."

"I have my mask and some airsickness bags, if that's what you mean."

"Certainly not," Jory huffed. "I meant the stupid number-two pencils."

"Don't worry. Actually, I feel pretty decent. I didn't go to chemo yesterday."

Jory stopped in her tracks halfway between the parking lot and the auditorium doors. "You what?"

"I skipped chemo. I told Dr. Rowan I'd be there Monday, but I didn't want to take a chance on lousing up the PSATs."

Incredulous, Jory demanded, "And he agreed to that?"

"He didn't have a choice. What was he going to do? Come to my house and pick me up bodily?"

"What did Michael say?"

"He doesn't know. And no one's going to tell him, is she?" Melissa threatened with a growl.

"I don't know why I'm supposed to cover for

you," Jory grumbled. "I'm always the one who gets caught."

Melissa touched Jory's arm at the door of the cavernous auditorium. "Because you're my friend. And because you know how much it means to me to score high on this test."

Jory didn't answer, but yanked open the door and preceded Melissa inside. Mrs. Watson rushed up to them. "Oh, Melissa, how good to see you."

Melissa couldn't help noticing the shock in her teacher's eyes when she saw her. "Thank you, Mrs. Watson." She slipped on the surgical mask.

"I've saved you special seats in the last row." Melissa followed Mrs. Watson keeping her eyes cast downward. She sat on the aisle and Jory sat next to her. "Every other chair, dear," Mrs. Watson directed, so Jory repositioned herself.

Melissa looked up cautiously, dipping the brim of her hat. The auditorium was almost full since the entire junior class was there to take the test. She was relieved to see that few kids had noticed her entrance. Most were whispering to friends or merely staring into space. Her stomach churned, but she knew it was from nerves. She had to score well on this test if her hopes for a Merit Scholarship were to be realized. The results would be sent to her in December, but it wouldn't be until the following September that principals would be notified as to which of their seniors were semifinalists. She rummaged in her purse for a mint, hoping to chase away the foul taste in her mouth. That was one side effect of her medications she could live without—the altered taste of food. Some days nothing tasted right.

Lincoln's principal sauntered across the stage in the front of the auditorium and made announcements about the exam. Feet shuffled. The materials were passed down each row, reminding Melissa of the day she'd taken the test for Brain Bowl. How long ago had that been? It felt like a hundred years.

On command, all the students opened the exam. She prayed she wouldn't get sick since she knew she'd be fighting the clock. She pulled her mask away from her face, took in a big gulp of air, then resettled the mask and started the test.

"So how'd you do?" Back in the safety of the car, it was the first remark out of Jory's mouth.

"I think I did okay. How about you?"

Jory grimaced and gripped the steering wheel, nosing the car out of the parking lot well in advance of the rest of the kids filing out of the auditorium. "It wasn't so tough."

"Thanks for getting me out in a hurry. I didn't want to have to talk to anybody and answer any dumb questions."

"No problem."

"Did I make you rush any answers?"

Jory blew air through her lips. "Get serious. What I didn't know, I guessed at. Big deal. I'm not the one who's so hot to go to college." She gave Melissa a studied look. "How are you feeling?"

Melissa grinned. "Pretty good. In fact, I feel good enough to stop for a milk shake. A chocolate one. Somehow, I've got this terrible craving for chocolate."

"Works for me. How about the Steak 'n Shake?" Jory named the restaurant that provided fifties-style curb service. "Then you won't have to go inside and try and drink through a hole in your mask."

"Let's go," Melissa told her friend. The grayness of the morning had been replaced by a weak wash of sunshine. Outside the air was still cool, so Jory kept the top up and the windows raised. Melissa fiddled with the radio dial until she found a song she liked.

At the drive-in restaurant, Jory parked to the far end despite a scowl from a waitress on roller skates who whizzed over to the car. "What'll it be, girls?"

"Two large chocolate shakes and one large order of fries."

The waitress eyed the expensive auto and muttered, "Big spenders."

"Tell the chef to go heavy on the grease on those fries," Jory called as the woman skated away. "And don't slip bringing it back."

Melissa giggled. "She's worried about her tip, you know. Two shakes and fries won't pay her rent."

"So let her take up brain surgery with the rest of the centerfolds working here."

When the food came, Melissa tasted it cautiously.

"Is it all right?" Jory wanted to know.

"Don't mind me. My medications sometimes give food a funny taste."

"And so?"

"And so this is delicious. Tastes just like liver."

"You're kidding." Jory's mouth dropped open, causing Melissa to laugh out loud.

"I'm kidding. It's good. Thanks."

They nibbled on the fries and listened to the music. "You know," Jory observed, "this is just like old times."

Melissa tapped the brim of her hat. "In some ways."

"It won't always be like this, Melissa. You're going to lick this thing."

"Thanks for the vote of confidence." Melissa straightened suddenly at the sight of a bronze-colored car. Brad Kessing parked his Firebird across the concrete median dividing the two parking areas. Brad was not alone. Melissa slouched low in the bucket seat of Jory's vehicle. "Let's split."

"But I'm not finished with my . . ." Jory's sentence trailed as she followed Melissa's line of vision. "Why that creep."

"Stop it, Jory." Melissa's tone sounded wooden. "He's a free agent. I have no claims on him."

"He's still a creep."

Curiosity gnawed at Melissa, and she peeked out the window for a better look at the girl with Brad. She was pretty, with wispy blond curls. "Do you know who she is?"

A guilty look crossed Jory's face that Melissa couldn't miss. "Sarah something or other."

"You've known about Brad and her for a long time, haven't you?"

"Not that long," Jory said with a self-conscious shrug. "A few weeks."

"It's all right you didn't tell me. I have no hold on Brad. He made me no promises."

"He really *did* ask me about you a few times. I mean he was really interested in how you were doing."

A sad smile turned up Melissa's mouth. "It's all right. You don't have to make me feel better about it." She set the milk shake on the car's console. "I think I'm finished with this thing. It's lost its flavor."

Jory flashed her lights, and when the waitress came she paid her. As she backed the car out, Melissa saw Sarah climb from Brad's Firebird, throwing him a provocative smile and words she couldn't hear. Brad, handsome and athletic, gave Sarah a thumbs-up signal, and Melissa fought a rising sadness.

The last thing she saw as they drove off was Sarah flipping her beautiful head of hair, laughing. "She's pretty," Melissa told Jory, straightening in her seat and adjusting her seat belt. "Pretty and perky—just Brad's type." To herself she added, *And healthy, too.*

Chapter Fourteen

December 10

    I don't think I've ever been so bored in my entire life. Funny, when Dr. Rowan told me that my lab results showed I'd gone into remission, I thought they'd break out the brass band. But it was purely routine. Business as usual. Now that I'm officially in remission, it's just a matter of getting my white count up enough to fight off normal germs before I can reenter the "real" world. Since it's almost time for the semester to end I guess it doesn't matter much. I'll just slip back into school in January . . . if such a thing is possible. I look really gross.

    Christmas is coming and I haven't bought anything. If it wasn't for Jory, I'd have nothing to put under the tree this year for Mom or Michael. Of course, Jory loved buying Michael's gift. She says she sniffed every men's cologne in the mall before picking one. She said the money I gave her was enough, but I know it wasn't. Anything that smells like that, in a glass bottle as fancy as the one it's in, couldn't have cost what I was able to afford. I made Michael get something really nice for Jory. He was a pain about it,

but he did find a sweater that's funky enough
for her. I hope she likes it.

Now that I'm on maintenance and don't
have to go to the clinic so often, I'm feeling
better. But I still get sick after every visit.
Will it ever go away? I see that little girl,
Rachael, sometimes. She's so cute and she
talks my ear off. Why do kids have to get
sick, anyway? Maybe it's one of the questions
I'll ask God when I see him . . .

Melissa stopped writing in her journal. The psy-
chiatrist had been right—there was something
therapeutic about putting down her thoughts and feelings. Although talking to herself on paper about everyday matters was now a habit, it still surprised her
when thoughts about God and faith and the whys of
sick kids slipped out. She sighed and and shut the
book. Time hung heavy for her. The days and nights
were too long, and she knew that so much introspec-
tion was getting her down.

She tucked the journal into her desk drawer and
studied her clock radio with a frown. Her mother
wouldn't be home from work for another hour.

The melodic chime of her phone made Melissa
jump. Annoyed by its ability to startle her, she
snapped "Hello."

"Melissa? Hi. It's Ric Davis."

Her hand squeezed the handset tightly and her
mouth went dry. "Why, Ric . . . How are you?"

"More to the point, how are you?"

"I'm doing all right. I look like a newborn baby,
the way my hair's coming back, though." She touched
the dark silky down on her head as she spoke. "But

'm taking the oral medications now and only going in or tests and some IV chemo. You know the routine."

"Yes, I know it. What have they got you on?" She old him and he said, "Watch that last one. It makes ou eat like a pig and before you know it, you'll weigh ton."

"I could use some meat on my bones," she con-essed, staring into the mirror on her dresser and wishing she hadn't. Her clothes still hung on her, and he baggy sweatshirt she wore did little to hide the hollow gauntness of her frame.

"Some meat, sure," he emphasized. "But that particular drug will make you bloated. That's what it did to me."

Melissa didn't like the course of the conversation. She didn't want to be told about more problems, more distortions to her body. Abruptly, she asked, "So what's new? Going home for Christmas?"

"Yeah, I am. I'm wrapping up exams tomorrow, hen catching a plane home. I'll be back after New Year's."

"Sounds like fun."

"If my prosthesis doesn't set off the metal detec-ors at the airport."

Same old, Ric, she thought. "It's nice of you to call and check on me, Ric."

"I told you when you were still in the hospital that I wanted to go out with you. I still do."

Her dry mouth felt like cotton. "I'm not sure I'm ready to face the world yet."

"You're going back to school aren't you?"

"Yes. But that's almost a month away. I . . . uh . . I'm hoping I look better by then."

"In other words, there's a guy you like and he'
been sort of cool since he found out you have cancer.

She would have dropped the phone if she hadn'
been gripping it so tightly, yet the uncanny accuracy
of his comment made her defensive. "That's not wha
it is."

"Come on, Melissa. It happened that way witl
me. Her name was Megan."

She thought about Brad and tan, healthy Sarah
Her shoulders drooped. "I know that the kids a
school will have to adjust to the new me when I go
back. After all, I look so different now." She raised he
chin and slipped in a note of defiance. "But I'm stil
me."

Ric's low-throated chuckle came through the line
"I know, Melissa. And that's the girl I'm interested ir
dating."

She felt herself softening toward him. Ric did un
derstand, and he had already traveled the road she
was about to take. "So call me when you get back to
campus. Okay?"

"You're on," he said. "Now take good care of your
self, and have a Merry Christmas."

"Thanks, Ric. You too." She hung up feeling a
wistful nostalgia she couldn't explain.

Later, when Jory stopped by and she'd told hei
about Ric's call, her friend asked, "Ric's older, isn'
he?"

"Nineteen."

"Thought you didn't like 'older men,'" Jory nee-
dled.

"Be kind, Jory. I don't feel very witty today."

"Well, do you want to date him?"

"I'm not exactly deluged with offers you know."

"Yeah, but that's going to change once things leve!

ut for you. In a few months, no one will even think of ou as having been sick."

"What do you do? Sit around and compare notes vith Michael? That's exactly what he says." Irritation had crept into her voice.

"I wish I could sit around and compare notes with aim." Jory rolled her eyes and reached for the bowl of popcorn resting between them on the floor of Melissa's living room.

Melissa pursed her lip. Why couldn't Jory and Michael and her mother understand how she felt about herself? Her body had turned on her. Without warning, it had begun making cancerous cells and changed all the rules of her life. "Forget it. If Ric calls again, I'll decide then if I want to date."

"You need to get your confidence back."

"You're right," Melissa said, resigned. "I don't feel like dating because I don't feel like a decent-looking girl any more."

Eagerly, Jory leaned forward, her green eyes dancing. "What do you say we retire the scarves and go wig shopping. I know just the place. It's private. The saleslady is sharp and knows her stuff. You'll love it. You can try on everything in the store. What do you think?"

"Mom told me I could get whatever I wanted for Christmas," Melissa said, trying hard to catch Jory's enthusiasm. "I guess I might as well start with new hair."

Two days later, Jory dragged her into a secluded salon, tucked away in a corner of the mall's most prestigious department store. The lights were bright, mirrors and wig stands lined the walls, and Styrofoam heads and round boxes clustered on shelves and pieces of furniture. A vanity table with chairs on ei-

ther side and a swivel mirror in its center dominated
the floor area. Settling into one of the chairs, a saleswoman with a soft southern accent and long, slim fingers jotted notes on a pad as she questioned Melissa
about her tastes. Without her mask, Melissa felt
somewhat exposed, but she was glad she didn't have to
wear it in public any longer.

The woman eyed her with keen, professional interest and noted, "If you want to go through these
swatches, you can show me the color that's closest to
your natural hair. And if you tell me a little about the
style, I can show you something so similar to your own
that you'll be hard-pressed to tell the difference between your real hair and your new wig." The idea that
she had an option hadn't occurred to Melissa. "Long
or short?" The woman asked.

"Oh, long," Jory interjected. "And dark. Melissa
had hair all the way down to her waist. And none of
this fake stuff either. Melissa wants real hair."

Nervously, Melissa licked her lips and shot Jory a
pleading glance. "Whose hair is this, anyway?" she
asked with a tense laugh.

The saleswoman intervened. "Natural human
hair that long would be very expensive and we'd have
to special-order it from the Orient. They seem to be
the only women growing long hair these days. Human
hair is also harder to maintain, and it's color can fade.
You can buy it," she added hastily, "but believe me,
synthetic hair is much less costly and just as attractive."

"No," Melissa said hastily. "I don't want long hair.
And I'm not so sure I want something just like I used
to have." She ignored Jory's surprised expression.

"Many women want a wig that most resembles

their natural hair, but the choice is yours. And we do have many choices," the clerk said gently.

"I have an opportunity to change my image, don't I? So why not?"

Quickly the woman crossed to the shelves and returned with a variety of wigs in a range of colors. "Would you like to be a blond?"

"They have more fun, right?"

She smiled and placed a saucy, curly wig on Melissa's head. The hairpiece felt warm and clung to her scalp, but the tight curls clustered about her face only emphasized the hollowness of her cheeks. "I don't think so," Melissa told her.

"How about this?" Jory asked from across the room, where she was searching the merchandise at random.

"That's our Dolly Parton look," the clerk said, settling the almost white, bouffant-style wig on Melissa. "We do a big business in theater and stage performers." One look in the mirror and Melissa cracked up.

"All you need is a guitar," Jory said, laughing hysterically.

Melissa glanced down at the front of her bulky knit sweater. "A guitar and two watermelons," she corrected. She turned to the saleswoman. "Maybe something a little less 'show biz.'"

Laughing herself, the clerk removed the wig and selected another, more sedate one. An hour and twenty wigs later, Melissa finally chose a thick chestnut fall with a little curl that hung just below her ears. It was soft to her touch, but felt odd, too. It was strange to run her fingers through the hair and not have it tug at her scalp. The saleswoman taught Melissa how to care for it, to clean and brush it and secure it to its Styrofoam head when not in use. Melissa paid for it, placing the crisp bills in the saleswoman's hand, then carried the box through the store, ignoring the festive twinkle of lights and decorated Christmas trees. Outside in the parking lot, she tugged her trench coat closer against a raw, gusty wind.

Beside her, Jory said, "It looks good on you."

"Sure." Melissa's teeth chattered slightly. "Almost like the real thing." They drove home in silence because Melissa wasn't sure she could talk without bursting into tears.

Michael made her model the hairpiece when they returned. His expression was reserved, studious. "It's . . . uh . . . different."

"Beats bald," she said tersely.

"I like it," Jory babbled. "Don't you think it was smart to go with a shorter look? I mean, we're the only ones who know about her real hair. This way, it just seems like she's cut it short. Even the color's just like her own . . ." Jory's animated voice trailed off and Melissa glanced at her. Her friend was looking straight at Michael and, as usual, was wearing her heart in her eyes.

Michael hooked his thumbs through the belt loops of his jeans. The sleeves of his navy blue sweater were pushed up, and Melissa noticed his forearms corded with muscle from hard physical labor. Melissa felt sorry that he had to work so hard. "Well, it's better than the haircut by Delaney," he finally said with a softness in his tone.

Rising to the gambit, Jory huffed, "I'll have you know that haircut was a work of art, Michael."

"More like graffiti," he fired back, good-naturedly.

Melissa stepped between them and held up her hands in mock surrender. "Please, I don't think I can referee another round. How about a truce?"

Michael slipped his arm around her shoulders and hugged her to him. "You win, Sis. By the way, you got some mail."

"Where?" Michael grabbed an oversize envelope from the kitchen counter and handed it to her. Melissa's heart hammered. Through the glassine window, she read her name, neatly typed by an impersonal computer in Illinois. "It's my PSAT scores."

"Aren't you going to open it?" Jory asked anxiously.

Melissa tore it open and Jory grabbed for the sheet labeled "Interpreting Your Score" while Melissa read the numbers on the printout. "Raw scores: Verbal 55, Math 41. Scaled scores: Verbal 64, Math 67. Selection index: 195. Percentile ranking: 98." She glanced up.

"You're a genius," Jory interpreted quickly. "According to this, ninety-eight percent of all high school juniors in the country scored below you." She paused before adding sheepishly, "Including me."

"You got your scores? You never said a word."

"What's to say? Only seventy-five percent of all juniors scored below me."

"But that's terrific." Melissa concentrated on Jory's scores because she still hadn't absorbed the impact of her own.

Michael had taken the information sheet from Jory and was reading it for himself. "You know what this means, don't you?" He didn't wait for a response. "It means you have a real shot at a Merit Scholarship."

Melissa had always assumed that the news would elate her. Hadn't that been her dream for over a year?

But instead, she felt strangely let down, out of sorts. The thing she'd wanted so badly, worked for for so long, seemed unreal and unrelated to her life right now. "Good for me," was all she could say. "I won't know until after the SATs next fall if I'm smart enough to advance," she told them.

"Yeah, but it says here '. . . about 50,000 high scorers will be given the opportunity to be identified to two colleges of their choice by the Merit Program in the spring.' You *have* picked two colleges worthy of taking you, haven't you?" Michael joked.

"Not yet," she hedged, her look warning Jory to keep quiet about Princeton. "When you have cancer, your options are different." She fled the kitchen, jerking the wig from her head.

In the living room she paused to stare at piles of Christmas decorations Michael had brought in from the garage. The boxes were frayed and tinsel hung sadly from one of them. He'd moved aside the easy chair and cleared a space for the tree. She stroked the synthetic hairpiece gathered in her fist. "Merry Christmas," she whispered to the pile of dark fibers. "Merry Christmas."

Chapter Fifteen

"Welcome back, Melissa. It's good to see you again."

Melissa acknowledged the greeting in the crowded halls as she had all the others her first day back in school. She waved and smiled at people, but she didn't feel it in her heart. She stopped in front of her locker and fumbled with the lock, concentrating so hard on the combination that she ran through it twice before she realized the locker was open.

"How's it going?" Jory's voice in her ear caused her to start.

"Fine," she lied.

"Everybody's asking about you . . ."

"I know," Melissa snapped, more sharply than she'd intended. "Geez, Jory. I feel like a freak. I can't even go to the girls' room without everyone staring, and when I walk into a classroom, there's instant silence. When I went into homeroom today, everything stopped and the entire class watched me walk to my desk. I felt like a murderer on death row walking to the electric chair." Melissa's blood raced with the intensity of her tirade, but having blasted off her pent-up emotions, she felt mollified. "Sorry," she said sheepishly. "I didn't mean to take it out on you."

"No problem," Jory shrugged. "The novelty will wear off as kids get used to having you back. Cancer's a

121

crummy thing to have happen, that's all. People just want to know how you're coping."

Melissa wanted to tell Jory that people's interest in her was ghoulish, similar to the chasing of ambulances, being drawn not out of compassion, but out of the morbid. Instead, she gazed into the hand mirror she'd hung on the inside of her locker door. Her face looked puffy, a side effect of the medicine Ric had warned her about. Her makeup looked unreal, too. *Why not?* she thought. *Fake face, fake smile, fake hair . . .* She touched the ends of the wig softly framing her face, and wished she'd opted for one with curls.

"Have you seen Brad yet?" Jory interrupted her dismal thoughts.

"No, not until sixth-period study hall. He's got soccer practice after school, so he won't be at Brain Bowl drill either." Truthfully, she was dreading seeing him. She looked so awful and she was acutely aware that he'd not contacted her once since that single phone conversation when she'd been in the hospital. And Jory had arranged for that.

"Will you be in the cafeteria for lunch?" Jory asked.

"Could we go out for lunch?"

"Sure. Where?"

"McDonald's . . . the drive-thru. We can eat in the car." Her tone turned pleading. "I can't make it through the rest of the day any other way."

Jory's wide green eyes swept her. "No problem. Meet me at my car."

The warning bell sounded and the halls emptied rapidly. "We're late," Melissa observed. "I'm sorry I made you late."

"Tardiness is my modus operandi," Jory said, with

a wave of dismissal. "I learned that phrase once in civics class. Does it impress you?"

"Deeply." Melissa squeezed her friend's arm gratefully. "Thanks, Jory. Thanks for everything." She hurried off, struggling to keep her throat from closing up with tears. At the door of her classroom, she squared her shoulders and entered, conscious that all eyes had turned in her direction. She passed down the aisle to her desk, hearing only brief snatches of whispered words. "Cancer . . ." the nameless voices said. "What a bummer . . ." and "Remember how pretty she was . . ."

Melissa arrived at study hall before anyone else and sat down quickly. At least this way, she could avoid an entrance. She could also watch for Brad.

When he came into the room, he was talking to another guy and didn't look up before sliding into his desk. She swallowed hard, absorbing him secretly with quick, stealthy glances.

His blond hair had darkened since the summer and it was longer, too, brushing his collar. A vivid turquoise sweater stretched across his broad shoulders. As always, his legs were too long for the cramped area beneath his desk. A flash of gold from his wrist caught her eye—an ID bracelet with solid gold links. She was torn between wanting him to turn around and yet hoping he wouldn't see her. For whatever reason, he never did, keeping his attention riveted on the pile of books in front of him. As a senior, he'd probably already chosen his college and wistfully, she wondered which one. There was so much she didn't know. So much she wanted to know.

At the Brain Bowl drill that afternoon, Melissa

was sharp. Mr. Marshall said, "You did well, Melissa. I'm very impressed."

"Thank you. I studied a lot over the break." She carefully avoided references to the hospital.

"It shows."

She was pleased by the teacher's praise, but didn't delude herself for a minute that she wasn't low person on the totem pole to make the final team. *I'll just have to work harder,* she told herself grimly as she hurried down the deserted halls to meet Jory, who was serving detention in the girl's locker room.

Melissa peeked inside and saw her snapping gum and doodling on her notebook while the gym teacher concentrated on paperwork. Jory waved her away, mouthing, "Fifteen minutes." Melissa nodded and eased out, hoping the teacher didn't catch Jory with gum in her mouth, or the punishment might stretch into another fifteen.

Feeling weary, Melissa deposited her load of books at her feet and lounged against the wall. She was mentally reviewing her day when the doors of the boys' locker room burst open, releasing a boisterous group of guys. Her eyes grew wide as Brad sauntered out. Seeing her, he stopped short. His blue eyes swept over her, then down the empty halls. *Trapped.* That's how he looked to her. Cornered and trapped.

"Uh—hi, Melissa."

She straightened automatically. "Hi." Her heart seemed wedged in her throat.

He took a few cautious steps in her direction, his eyes darting away from hers. "How have you been?"

One of the guys called, "You coming, Kessing?"

"In a minute," he said. "Wait for me outside."

Another one scrutinized Melissa. "Don't take all

day, man. I told my old lady I'd be home right after practice."

Once they had gone, Melissa felt the silence of the corridors press around her. Brad heaved his books on his hip and gestured with his free hand. "So, it's good to see you back. I looked for you in study hall, but missed you."

Liar. "I was there."

"How was Brain Bowl? Did the drill go okay? I hate missing it, but Coach is real strict about soccer practice—if you miss one, you don't start in the next game."

"Brain Bowl went fine." She noticed his hair, still damp from the shower, making his shirt collar wet.

He licked his lips. "You . . . uh . . . look real good, Melissa. How're you feeling?"

"All right."

"I guess it's been a while since we've talked."

"Yeah. A while." She hoped the bitterness didn't sound in her tone. She wanted to shout, *You didn't call me, Brad. Not even once. Why?*

"Your hair's different. Too bad you had to cut it short."

Her fingers toyed with the soft ends of the wig, which felt artificial and not like "real" hair as the saleslady had insisted. "I figured it was time for a change."

Brad fidgeted. "Did you have a good Christmas?"

"One of the best."

"That's good."

She let her eyes fall on the ID bracelet. "Christmas gift?"

"From my grandfather."

"The Rhodes Scholar?"

"One and the same." He smiled but shifted nervously to his other foot. "Are you . . . um . . . you know, all right now?"

She pinned him with a look. "If you mean do I still have leukemia, yes, I do. I'm still on medication, but I'm in remission." He knitted his brow and she could read the anxiety on his face. For some perverse reason, she wanted him to squirm. She wanted to punish him for not calling her. For not sending a card. For everything.

Brad took one step closer, reminding her of a childhood game. *Simon Says, take one tiny baby step.* "Melissa . . . I really do want you to be okay. I wish . . . you were . . . well . . ." His voice broke and for the briefest moment she thought he might reach out and stroke her hair.

Panicked, she pressed closer to the wall, feeling its hardness against the small of her back. She remembered summer sunshine and bright green leaves and cool, quiet water laced with goldfish and blossoms. She recalled how Brad had undone her braid and raked his fingers through her tangled hair, gathering it into handfuls and then letting it fall against her skin. She knew she couldn't stand to have him touch her hairpiece. For one desperate second, she held her breath and mutely challenged him with her eyes, saying, "Don't touch." She wasn't sure why, but she wanted him to have this last illusion. She *needed* him to have it.

Brad dropped his hand and backed away. "I gotta go. The guys are waiting."

"Sure." She tossed her head, longing to feel her cascading hair against her shoulders and back.

"See you at Brain Bowl drill."

"See you."

He retreated down the hall and she deliberately

turned away so she didn't have to watch him go. Moments later, Jory burst through the girls' locker room doors. "Geez! What a drag! Sorry you had to wait."

"No problem," Melissa said, scooping up her books. "Ready to head home?"

"You better believe it." Jory cocked her head. "Are you feeling all right? You look a little pale."

"I'm tired, that's all. It's been a long day."

Together, they trudged outside into the pale winter sunshine and biting fresh air. "Free!" Jory exclaimed, lifting her face skyward.

Free. Melissa wondered if she'd ever feel free again. "Want to come over for dinner?" she asked, remembering that Jory's parents had flown to the Bahamas that morning on some real estate deal.

"Am I invited? Will Michael be there?"

"Aren't we choosy?"

"Just wondering how to dress, grungy or designer jeans." Jory's smile was brief. "Not that he notices either way. But it's fun to hope."

Across the parking lot, Melissa saw Brad's Firebird gathering speed, heading for the highway that ran in front of Lincoln High. Her hopes for him had fled. The wind ruffled her hair, blowing it across her mouth. She pushed it back, but the taste lingered, dry and false.

Chapter Sixteen

After supper, Melissa and Jory sat together on Melissa's bed, pouring over homework. Melissa felt distracted and her mind kept wandering. It must have been obvious because Jory finally asked, "What's the matter? You keep staring off into space. Where's the scholar who's going to knock the world on its butt?"

Melissa managed a half smile. "I couldn't knock a fly off a wall."

"Level with me, Melissa. What's wrong?"

"It was harder going back to school than I thought it would be. Everything's different."

"I told you people would stop talking about you in a few days. It's no big deal."

"I saw Brad while I was waiting for you." Her voice sounded small.

Jory closed her book and nodded thoughtfully. "So, that's it."

"Not just Brad," Melissa balled her hands into fists, searching for a way to explain her feelings. "It's what Brad represents."

"Which is?"

"Jory, remember when we didn't have anything more complicated to think about than what color shirt to go with a pair of pants? Or who was taking who to a party?"

Jory frowned. "Is there a party you want to go to with Brad?"

Agitated, Melissa shook her head and began to pace her room. "Fat chance that Brad Kessing will ever ask me anyplace."

"You mean you don't think he'll ask you for a date?" Jory pulled up her legs and rested her chin on her knees. "Is this what's got you in such a tailspin? You've finally decided that something matters besides grades, but now the guy you were 'sort of interested in' might be interested in someone or something else?"

"Hardly." Melissa locked eyes with her friend. "I have cancer, Jory. People treat me like I'm some sort of *untouchable*. What guy is going to date me?"

"Ric?" Jory ventured.

"What *regular* guy?" Annoyance edged Melissa's question.

"So what?" Jory shrugged. "Being asked out is nothing. I go out all the time and mostly it's dullsville."

Of course Jory got asked out, Melissa thought. She was fun and full of energy and always ready for a good time. "But I *want* to be asked. Who wants me? Or my cancer?" Melissa's words hung in the air between them. The silence was so deep that Melissa could hear the faint sounds of the TV coming from the living room, where her mother was watching it.

"I know what you're talking about, Melissa. But why should it matter now? Four months ago all you wanted was a college scholarship and no involvements. I practically dragged you to meet Brad. Now, you're that far away from college." She gestured with her thumb and forefinger. "You're getting better and stronger every day. Why should Brad matter so much to you now?"

"Because four months ago I didn't have leukemia.

And Brad looked at me like I was beautiful. Today he looked at me like . . . like I was a leper. Like if he touched me, he would catch it."

Jory's voice grew very quiet. "That's his problem."

"No. It's my problem, too. Because it's happening to *me*, Jory. Not to some stranger, but to Melissa Austin."

Melissa parked Michael's truck in the hospital lot, entered the outpatient oncology clinic, and weaved through the maze of children and toys scattered on the floor of the waiting room. It always amazed her to see how many children had cancer. Some were bald, others looked perfectly healthy, yet what touched her most was not how they looked, but how much they acted like normal kids. They fought over toys, they pitched tantrums, they shed tears over hurt feelings. Their mothers often sat stony and withdrawn, but the children never forgot to be children.

Since she'd come for only a blood workup, Melissa walked straight into DeeDee Thomas's office. The diminutive, dark-haired nurse offered a beleaguered smile. "Hi, Melissa. It's a madhouse around here today, but I can work you up in a few minutes. Do you mind waiting?"

"Of course I do. But I will. Just for you."

The nurse poked her playfully. "You're too kind. Oh, incidentally, there's someone in the chemo room who's been asking for you, Rachael Dove. I told her you'd be in today and she's been waiting for you ever since."

Melissa felt a softening sensation. "She's such a doll. How's she doing?"

Nurse Thomas's hands kept busy, sorting through piles of paper on her overloaded desk. "Now where's that form? Ah . . . Here it is . . . Second remissions are even tougher to achieve and maintain. It's a battle, but she's holding her own."

The nurse's honesty caused a chill to go through Melissa. She said with brightness, "I'll go visit her now, and you can come get me when you're ready to draw blood." She walked quickly down the hall to the chemo room—the contour chairs and IV stands seemed all too familiar to her.

Rachael lay in one of the chairs, curled on her side and coloring. "Hi, Rachael."

The tiny girl glanced up and gave her a toothy smile. "Hi, Melissa. I'm coloring this just for you." Melissa looked at the scene from *Cinderella*. "This is Cinderella after her fairy godmother dressed her in her ball gown. Do you like it?"

"It's beautiful. I like pink."

"I've still got some more to do." Rachael sounded disappointed.

"Oh, I'll be here a while. You can finish it."

The little girl grinned. Her skin looked paper thin, and she'd lost all her hair. Her blue eyes seemed too large for her tiny face. "I picked this page," the child explained, "because you're all grown up and can go to balls and dances and stuff like that."

"I'd rather read a book."

Rachael giggled. "I'd rather go to a ball and meet a prince."

Deciding to change the subject, Melissa asked, "So how's your baby sister?"

Rachael made a face. "She cries a lot. But sometimes Mommy lets me hold her and give her a bottle. It was fun till she wet on me."

"Isn't that just like a baby? Do you like her any better than you did the last time we talked?"

"I guess so . . ." Rachael admitted with a sheep-ish shrug. "Sometimes she smiles at me. There!" Rachael announced triumphantly. "All finished."

Melissa reached down, took the book, and care-fully tore out the page. "I'm going to hang this in my bedroom, and every time I look at it, I'll think of you."

The child beamed. She reached over to a small metal table and fished a clump of red curls off the top. "See what Mommy bought me? It's my new hair."

"So it is. Why'd you pick red?"

"Because I watch *Annie* on the VCR all the time. It's my favorite movie. Will you help me put it on?"

Melissa nestled the wig on Rachael's head. "You look just like a little movie star."

"I do? Justin Malone in Sunday school says I look like a clown."

"He's just jealous. You look lovely."

"I want to be a movie star when I grow up. What do you want to be?"

Melissa felt herself stiffen. A million thoughts tumbled through her head. High school graduation, college, her name on a brass nameplate. Would she see them all? "I've always wanted to be a lawyer," she said.

"You do? But you're so pretty. You could be a movie star." Touched, Melissa stooped down and hugged the child to her. "Thank you, Rachael. That's the nicest thing anyone's said to me in ages."

DeeDee Thomas leaned into the room. "I'm ready for you, Melissa."

"Coming," she said. "You take care, Rachael, and I'll see you again real soon. Thanks for the picture."

"I wish you were my sister," she said.

"I am, Rachael," Melissa said. "Because of all the

things we share, I *am* your sister. Don't ever forget that, okay?"

The Brain Bowl session hadn't gone well and Melissa knew it. She'd been slow on the buzzer and twice her mind had gone blank. She assumed it was because Brad was at the drill. The minute Mrs. Watson released the team, Melissa bolted for the door, eager to get away as quickly as possible.

"Melissa! Wait up!" Mrs. Watson's voice hailed her as she hurried out into the bright wintry afternoon. She reluctantly stopped and turned to the teacher. Forcing a smile, she said, "Yes, Mrs. Watson. What's up?"

"Nothing much. It's just the first opportunity I've had to talk to you since you've returned to school. I wanted to discuss Brain Bowl with you. You seemed a bit off today."

Is that what her teacher wanted? To criticize her performance? "Sorry. I know I've done better in other drills."

"Yes, you have. What was wrong?"

"Nothing. I'll do better tomorrow."

"The school board has scheduled the Brain Bowl round-robin between area high schools for the week following spring break in April."

"It has?"

"That means we'll be choosing our final panel the week before the round-robin match."

Melissa added up the remaining time. There were two and a half months until the panel would be chosen. "Why tell me this now?"

"I want you on it."

The teacher's forthright honesty caused Melissa to raise her eyebrow. "And I want to be on it."

Mrs. Watson smiled. "I didn't start this project to fail, Melissa. I didn't think you had either."

The insinuation annoyed her. "I didn't. I had a bad day, that's all. Am I the only one who can't have a bad day?"

Mrs. Watson studied Melissa for a long moment. "I want a winning team, and you're one of the best in our group."

Melissa was confused, unable to grasp the purpose of the conversation. "Is this a pep talk? I have every intention of making the team. I've probably worked harder than anybody for a spot. I can pull my own weight if I make the team, so don't feel you have to carry me."

"We *can't* carry you. So please don't stop working this close to the final selection process."

An inkling of Mrs. Watson's objective began to drift through to Melissa. She thought about the four other teachers responsible for choosing the team— Mr. Marshall, of course; Dean Crane; Mr. Wilson, the assistant principal; and Miss Judd, a science teacher. Counting Mrs. Watson, there was a total of five, so there could be no deadlocks on their votes. "Do the other faculty advisors think that my cancer may affect my ability to perform?" When Mrs. Watson said nothing, Melissa added, "It won't, you know. I've missed a lot, but I can do it."

"I know you can," Mrs. Watson said kindly.

"But some don't, is that what you're saying?"

Mrs. Watson touched Melissa's arm. "Prejudice isn't limited to race or religion, Melissa. I won't belabor the point." She waved her hand in dismissal. "But please, keep pouring yourself into this effort.

Now, remember, this conversation was between us girls, and I never would have said anything unless I wasn't pulling for you one hundred percent." She backed toward the faculty parking lot. "Tomorrow, Melissa . . . give it everything you've got."

Melissa watched Mrs. Watson hurry away, not sure whether she felt encouraged or defeated. Her teacher liked her and seemed to be on her side. But who wasn't on her side, and why? With a weary sigh, she crossed the vacant parking lot, unable to deal with it at that moment. Suddenly she heard someone calling her name and saw a guy leaning out of a blue van. She took a deep breath, recognizing Ricter Davis.

Chapter Seventeen

"Surprised to see me?" Ric asked as Melissa approached the van.

"Very surprised."

His face had filled out and his hair was stylishly cut, but his eyes were as dark and soul-piercing as she remembered. "Hop in," he said.

The van was carpeted in blue and outfitted with a small table and cushioned benches. "Looks like a home on wheels," she told him.

He chuckled. "In case I don't pay my dorm bill, I'll always have a place to stay."

His jeans hid his artificial leg, and she looked away immediately, afraid he'd think she was staring. "How did you find me?"

"I watched the school empty and kept an eye out for the pretty girls. I'd almost given up."

"I had Brain Bowl drill."

He glanced to the side. "Actually, I've waited for you before, but you always seemed to be with that girlfriend of yours."

"Jory." Melissa wasn't sure if she was flattered or not. "You could have called and come by my house."

He ignored her comment. "And then I saw you out front once with some blond-haired guy who looked pretty important to you." Her cheeks flushed, remembering how she and Brad had attempted to sidestep each other but wound up nearly colliding. "So I was right. He *is* important," Ric said when she didn't respond.

His condescending tone was irritating. "Ric, this is really silly. There're a hundred guys at Lincoln High."

"But only one you care about?"

She leaned forward, suddenly angry. "I think I resent this. You have no right skulking around the school, spying on me."

He drove with one hand and reached over and squeezed her shoulder with the other. His tone was apologetic. "I was just checking out my competition, Melissa. A guy has a right to know what he's up against."

"There is no competition," she said icily. "Brad Kessing is nothing to me."

Ric's grin was wide. "Good. Then there won't be any obstacles to our relationship, right?"

"We have no relationship," she told him, wishing he'd never come for her.

"I hope we will, Melissa," he said.

It seemed to Melissa that dating Ric was inevitable. And once she got over her initial animosity toward him, she really did have a good time with him. Her mother was hesitant at first. "He's older than you," she'd said. "I'd rather see you date some boy from your junior class." Melissa didn't have the heart to remind her that most boys from her school avoided girls with cancer.

Michael, however, was more adamant. "Why the hell is he interested in a sixteen-year-old? Can't he get girls his own age?"

"He likes me. Is that a crime?"

"He's almost my age, for God's sake."

"You're not my father, Michael. I'm old enough to choose my own dates."

"If he comes on to you . . ."

"Forget it. He's really just a friend."

Jory, on the other hand, had been philosophical about the matter. "I think you should date him and have a good time. Go enjoy yourself, but don't forget: I want details of every date, every party. Do I make myself clear?"

Melissa did tell Jory everything, but she also wrote in her journal.

> *February 20*
>
> *It's been a month since Ric and I first went out—a fast month, too. I like being with him and it makes me even more positive that I want to go away to college. He took me up to his dorm room and I met his roommate, Doug, and Doug's girlfriend, Cheri. Ric used a special knock before we went inside. It's funny, the way everyone's so casual about sex. It still makes me a little uptight. Ric and I aren't doing it, of course, but everyone just assumes we are, and I guess there's nothing I can do about that.*
>
> *Ric's frat parties get crazy at times. I don't drink because of my medications, and when you're the only sober person in a roomful of bombed people, it's weird. Ric drinks some, but never as much as the other guys, and if things get too wild, we leave. Last Saturday night they had a toga party and some guy stripped naked, so Ric got me out fast. Jory would be having a blast, but I'd hate to see her waste herself that way.*

> *Lincoln seems so tame by comparison.*
> *Brain Bowl is still my top priority. It hardly*
> *bothers me anymore to be around Brad.*
> *Maybe because I have someone else to con-*
> *centrate on, or maybe because I know it*
> *can't work out and that Brad still can't ac-*
> *cept me because I'm less than perfect. Ric*
> *accepts me, but sometimes I wonder what it*
> *is I really want. I like Ric, but . . .*

Melissa did not write in her journal about the
first time Ric kissed her because it would have seemed
too juvenile and because the kiss was hard and deep,
serious and a little rough. He tasted faintly of beer,
and her heart thudded like a jackhammer. She didn't
want him to know how limited her experience was in
that area, so she returned his kiss with far more passion than she felt. He pulled away, studied her briefly,
then kissed her again, this time more lightly. He said,
"You give me hope, Melissa."

"Hope for what?" She was grateful for the surrounding cover of the night so that he couldn't see the
faint tremors in her hands.

"For us, of course."

"I thought we were just having fun, Ric." Rock
music drifted from the fraternity house as they stood
under the sprawling oak tree on the front lawn.

"We are. But there's fun and there's fun."

She brushed aside his innuendo. "And I thought
you were attracted to my fine mind."

He chuckled and locked his arms around her
waist. "If there's one thing I've learned because of having cancer, it's to go after what you want in life."

"Why?"

"Because life's too short to stand around and wait for things to come your way."

She leaned into his palms, which rested in the small of her back. "Are you ever going to forgive life for dealing you cancer?"

"What's that supposed to mean?" His eyes narrowed in the moonlight.

"Ever since we first met, you've seemed really mad about what's happened to you. Why are you so angry all the time, Ric?"

"Why aren't you angrier?" He fired back.

"I am angry. Every time I go to the clinic and see those little kids and know what we're all going through together, I get very mad. But being mad doesn't change it."

"And being so accepting doesn't make it any easier," he challenged.

"I don't think I'm accepting of it, Ric. I'm not sure what I am about it."

"I know one thing you are," he said, his voice softer, smoothing over the anger that had reared between them.

"What?" She asked suspiciously.

"You're pretty." He brought his mouth to hers.

She caught her breath. "Don't do that."

"Why?" He traced the outline of her lips with his finger. "Sometimes I think this is all there is, Melissa. Feeling, hearing, tasting, seeing . . . What else can there be?"

She slipped from his grasp and waited for her pulse to stop racing, her blood to stop pounding in her ears. "I don't know what else there is, but I just think there's more."

His expression grew cynical. "Well, even if there is 'more,' this is where I want to start—with what I can touch and hold on to." He took her by the waist again and pulled her against him. She felt the hard outline of his body against the length of hers. Where their legs touched, she sensed his prosthesis through her jeans, and Ric relaxed his hold, knowing that she felt it. "Sometimes I forget my leg isn't there," he said. "Even a year after the amputation, I can still feel pains in my leg, still feel my foot. Ghost pains they call it."

Eager to help him forget, she said quickly, "I remember my hair in the same way. I sometimes reach to lift it when I sit down like I used to do so it wouldn't get caught on the back of a chair. And when I brush my wig, I often drop the brush because I expect my hair to be longer. Just for a moment I wonder why it isn't. Then I remember."

Ric fingered the tips of the wig. "This doesn't feel false," he whispered, burying his face in the side of her neck. "And it smells like you. Like fresh flowers."

The tingling sensation started in the pit of her stomach and diffused through her body with the warmth of his breath on her skin. "Thank you."

His mouth found hers again and this time his kiss was long and slow. She slipped her arms around his neck and let him stroke the contours of her body. She felt like satin inside. "We're a lot alike, Melissa."

He'd told her the same thing months before, when they'd been in the hospital. At the time, she'd resented the comparison. Now, she agreed with him. Their illness bound them together with invisible bands and they *were* alike. More alike than she and Brad would ever be. "Let's go inside," she said to him while her mind swirled and spun with the sensations his touch was arousing.

"All right," he said, his voice husky. "But I won't

always let you back off this way, Melissa. I'm not some high school kid, and I know what I want."

Melissa understood, but she didn't know what she wanted. She only knew she *wanted*. Deep inside her heart, she wanted.

"So how's college life?" Jory asked, taking a bite of apple.

"Why do you ask?"

"We never talk about you and Ric, that's all. I'm curious."

Melissa picked at the thick pile carpet in Jory's family room, ignoring the VCR movie that blared in the background. "There's not much to talk about."

"Come on, Melissa. You can talk to me. I'm not your mother. Haven't I spilled my guts about every date I've had this year? I expect the same courtesy from you."

Melissa smiled. "I don't know what you want to hear. I've told you all about the frat parties. I've told you where he takes me, what we do."

"But not how you *feel*," Jory said. "Do you care about him?"

"In a way," Melissa said.

"Ugh! You talk but you say *nothing*!"

"It's a good trait for a lawyer to have," Melissa joked. She knew she was putting Jory off and it bothered Melissa because they'd shared everything over the years. But these were thoughts and feelings she'd never known before, until Ric had brought them out. She couldn't talk it out, she couldn't share it, not even with her best friend. Jokingly, she raised her right hand and said, "I solemnly swear to tell Jory Delaney all my future plans from this day forth, so help me Hannah."

* * *

By the middle of March, the Brain Bowl drills were going like clockwork. Melissa and Brad and a science whiz named Lyle Vargas were the backbone of the team. She hadn't really known Lyle until Brain Bowl started, but she liked him. He was not only sensitive to her, but he seemed to like Jory, and Melissa thought they would make a nice couple if only she would give him the time of day.

Melissa was sure that the Lincoln High Brain Bowl team had a shot at advancing through the round-robin. Following a grueling practice session in late March, Melissa trudged out onto the grassy area in front of the school and looked around for Ric's van. It wasn't parked in its usual place, which meant he was late. She crossed her legs and dropped to the ground, running her palm over the spring growth of fine green grass. The soft blades reminded her of the hair sprouting beneath her wig.

The sun beat warmly on her shoulders, and she could smell the rich, loamy earth she sat on. She saw someone approaching and squinted. The girl stopped a short distance from where Melissa was sitting.

Melissa tried to place the face. *Sarah*. The girl waved, and a bronze Firebird pulled up alongside of her. But it wasn't the car or its driver that caught Melissa's eye. It was the gleaming gold ID bracelet locked on Sarah's wrist. Sarah was Brad's girl.

Chapter Eighteen

Brad drove off and a lump wedged in her throat. "This is stupid!" she said out loud, standing and dusting her jeans furiously. Hadn't she known for months about Sarah and Brad? It was silly for her to react to it.

A horn blew and Ric hailed her. She jumped into the van, slamming the door hard. "Who rattled your cage?" Ric asked.

"No one. It was a long day."

"Brain Bowl didn't go well?"

"I said it was a long day. Don't go reading something into nothing."

Ric shrugged and pulled away from the curb so fast that the tires squealed. "How about a hamburger?"

"Mom's expecting me for dinner."

"How about going out later to the library at the university? I've got a research paper to get moving on."

"I need to spend some time at home. Mom's starting to get on my case about going out all the time."

"You're avoiding me."

She gritted her teeth. "I just need some time to myself, Ric. That's all." Without warning, he pulled the van onto a small, dusty road that wound its way into some woods. "Where are you going?" she snapped. "I told you I needed to get home."

He ignored her until they reached a clearing and he shut off the engine. Opening her door he hauled her out. "Come on. Let's walk."

"Ric . . . please, I don't want to walk."

Taking her elbow, he led her along, past trees dripping with Spanish moss, toward a river, where he stopped and turned her to face him. "It's nice out here, Melissa. I sometimes come here to study and think."

Still angry, she took a few deep breaths before scanning her surroundings. Wild azalea bushes burst with fuchsia and pink blossoms, and water gurgled over rocks. "You're right. It's very pretty out here."

He lifted her chin and looked hard into her eyes. "I'm sorry you had a bad day."

"I overreacted. Forget it."

"But you still don't want to tell me about it?"

"There's nothing to tell. Honest."

He let it drop and Melissa was grateful. They stood in the clearing, quiet except for the sounds of the woods. Ric finally broke the silence, his voice hesitant and gentle. "Melissa, I want to ask you something. I was going to wait till Saturday, but I'm going to ask you now."

Suddenly she was alert. Her mouth went dry, but she forced some levity. "Ask away."

"Spring break's coming up."

"I know."

"Some of the guys from the house and the dorm floor are planning a trip down to Sarasota to spend a few days on the beach."

"I thought everyone went to Fort Lauderdale."

He grinned. "Highly overrated. Who wants to be stepping over bozos from Michigan and Ohio?" He brushed a wisp of her hair off her cheek and the gesture moved her. Ric never thought twice about her hair being a wig. "Doug's aunt has a place on Sanibel Island and he's taking Cheri there. Doug wants me to come along. And I want you to come with me."

Startled, she stared into his dark, coal-colored eyes. She knew what he was asking. She dropped her gaze and stared at the ground, where she unearthed a rock with the toe of her shoe. "I . . . I don't know . . ."

"I want to make love to you, Melissa. I want to sleep with you and wake up with you." He'd slipped his hands into the back pockets of his jeans but he somehow made her feel as if he were holding her.

"Ric . . . I . . . just can't take off for a weekend. What would I tell my mother? Michael?" She tried to swallow her rising panic.

"If you asked, I know your friend Jory would cover for you."

He'd already thought about the details for her, but she shook her head. "I don't know . . ."

Then Ric touched her, taking her gently by the shoulders. "You don't have to answer now. But will you think about it?"

"Ric . . . I don't—" She stopped, groping for the right words. "I mean . . . I've never . . ."

"I know you haven't, Melissa. But when you do, I want it to be with me."

Her cheeks burned, not from modesty, but from the overwhelming emotions she felt. Hadn't she wondered about what making love would be like? Hadn't she read passages in books that told how it felt? Watched old movies that aroused romantic feelings? "I don't know . . ."

He unbuttoned the top button of her blouse and gently ran his fingertips over her skin. Her knees went weak and she thought her heart might explode. "I've always thought you were pretty . . . from the first time I saw you. You were sitting in that hospital bed and you were combing your hair. That beautiful hair . . ."

She took a step backward, surprised that her legs could support her. Her brain whirled back to some long ago conversation, and she asked, "Who was Megan?"

Ric let his hands drop. "Why do you ask?"

"You mentioned her once. I wondered at the time, but didn't ask."

"She was just a girl I was dating when I was first diagnosed."

"And?"

"And she couldn't handle it." His expression darkened and his mouth pressed into a hard line.

She thought of Brad. Big and blond and so totally attractive to her. "Why can't anyone ever handle it?" she asked, but she didn't expect an answer. She raised her hand and laid her palm on Ric's cheek. "I will think about it, Ric. I'll think about it very hard."

He turned her palm and kissed it. "Two weeks," he told her. "We'll leave the weekend after next."

"You awake, Mom?" Melissa peeked into her mother's bedroom. Mrs. Austin was reading, propped up with pillows, a pile of file folders scattered over the bed.

She smiled and pushed her reading glasses on top of her head. "Come on in, honey." She shoved aside the folders, making a place for Melissa to sit. "This is a nice treat. To what do I owe the honor of such a visit?"

Melissa curled onto the bed and shrugged. "No reason. Do I need one?"

"You never needed one before. Actually, I've missed your visits. Remember how you'd always come in after dates and fill me in? And we'd pig out on cookies and milk?"

Melissa remembered. So much had changed for her over the past six months. "I guess most of it sounded pretty stupid."

"*Au contraire* . . . it kept me young." Melissa allowed a comfortable silence to stretch between them. Finally, her mother asked, "Got a problem?"

"No. Why do you ask?"

"Between school and Ric, you're very busy, honey. Is everything going all right for you?"

Melissa felt her inner defenses go up. She wasn't sure why she'd come into her mother's room. She certainly couldn't bare her soul about Ric's invitation to spend the weekend with him. "Everything's fine, Mom. Don't make a big deal out of a simple little nighttime visit." Melissa felt guilty for sounding short. "I was lonesome, that's all."

"No need to feel lonely. I'm always here."

Melissa nodded. "Yes. You're always here." She longed to tell her mother about Ric. Longed to have her tell her what to do. She'll say no, she thought. It was a mother's place to say no to such things. But I have leukemia, her reason argued. I might never face this choice again.

"Is this a private party or can anyone come?" Michael asked.

"Boy, this is my lucky night," Mrs. Austin said with a warm smile. "Both my kids at once. Come share the bed," she said.

"Can't—I'm too grubby," Michael said, sinking to the floor. "So what's up?"

"Nothing," Melissa said. "Just girl talk." Her heart went out to him. "How's your balloon club?"

"You make it sound like a kiddie club." His grin was impish.

"That's what I get for making polite conversation with a man." She emphasized the last word as if it were a dirty one.

"Watch it, woman, or I may gag and tie you and take you up with me this weekend."

"Thanks for the invitation," she said, "but I hardly ever have a good time when I'm nauseated."

The three of them laughed and Mrs. Austin tossed off the covers. "Cookies," she said. "This occasion calls for cookies and milk. You two wait right here and I'll bring back a tray."

Michael held her robe and Melissa watched them, feeling how much she loved them both. She remembered the early days of her diagnosis and hospitalization. The angry words she'd hurled at her mother and the way Michael had always retreated from any conversation about her illness. None of them had really accepted it yet—especially her brother—but right now, in the comfort of her mother's room, it seemed that nothing could hurt them.

Melissa shook her head to clear it. She would think about Ric and cancer and choices tomorrow. Tonight she would be the little girl who used to sit on her mother's bed and share her heart's secrets.

"Lots of cookies," she called. "Chocolate ones. And make sure the milk is real cold."

Melissa sensed a tension in the clinic. DeeDee Thomas was a jangle of nerves, dropping the tourniquet she was trying to tie around Melissa's arm, contaminating the sterile needle and having to pop open another.

"What's wrong?" Melissa asked, watching DeeDee hunt for a vein along the inside of her arm.

"Just a typical crazy day. Don't mind me."

"It's always crazy around this place. But today seems crazier and you're kind of distracted. Are you sure nothing's wrong?"

DeeDee looked up, half-smiling, and her eyes looked tired. "I was working half the night upstairs in oncology. Then two people called in sick down here and someone had to fill in. I'm wiped out, that's all."

"My blood work's still looking good," Melissa said, trying to make conversation.

"Good. I want you to be well, Melissa. I want all of you to be well," DeeDee said.

"All of us?"

"The kids. All the kids." She gestured vaguely and taped a cotton ball across Melissa's vein.

Usually when her lab work was complete, Melissa tore out of the place, trying to escape the anti-septic smells and reminders of this other world she belonged to. But today she hesitated. "Know what?" she said to DeeDee. "I think I'll go up and visit the floor. Dr. Rowan said that it was a good idea to go up every once in a while so that the really sick kids can see that that part doesn't last forever."

"No, Melissa. Don't go up. Not today."

DeeDee's sharp directive surprised her. "Why not?"

The nurse's eyes were evasive. "It's just a bad day up there."

An icy cold feeling seized Melissa's heart. "What's wrong? What's happened?"

DeeDee straightened and absently tried to tuck

some wayward hair behind her ear. "We had a death," she said. "It was a long fight, but we lost it."

"Who?" Melissa felt her stomach churn.

DeeDee sagged. "The little girl, Rachael Dove. We put her on a respirator yesterday, but today there was no brain activity. We turned off the machine less than an hour ago."

Chapter Nineteen

The ride in the elevator was smooth and silent. Melissa shivered at the haunting familiarity of the oncology floor. It was as if she'd walked into a time warp. Everything was exactly as she had left it months before. Almost.

The atmosphere was subdued. Nurses moved efficiently, their voices softened, their expressions grim. Melissa hadn't expected the loss to have affected all of them so obviously. She'd figured that they must be used to it, conditioned to it. Yet grief was etched clearly in their faces. She'd never thought of them as anything other than trained professionals, just doing a job, but she saw them now as people, *grieving* people.

She stood near the nurses' station, momentarily confused, unable to decide what to do, where to go. Which room had been Rachael's? She wanted to ask one of the nurses, but couldn't bring herself to approach anybody. They might ask why she wanted to know, and she had no reason. She began to walk slowly down the hall painted with a gay circus theme, glancing into doorways, inexplicably drawn. She didn't want to go. She *had* to go.

She knew she'd found the right room the second she peeked inside. Machines banked one wall, and a hospital bed stood in the center of the floor, empty. Melissa entered, her heart pounding so hard, she felt sick to her stomach.

"Can I help you?" The unexpected voice caused Melissa to jump. "I'm sorry. I didn't mean to scare you."

The girl was about Melissa's age, dressed in a pink striped uniform, preparing to make the bed. "I-It's all right. I didn't think anybody was in the room."

"My name's Laura Lopez. I work here as a volunteer."

Melissa felt disappointed that she wasn't alone. "I'm Melissa Austin."

Laura shook out the sheet and smoothed it across the forlorn-looking bed. "My father's a doctor here at the hospital and my brother's a physical therapist. I guess you might say this place is in my blood." Melissa watched Laura expertly tuck in the corners of the sheet. "Did you know Rachael?" Laura asked.

"Yes. We sometimes had our clinic appointments at the same time."

Laura straightened up from her bed-making. "Oh—you're *Melissa*."

"Yes."

"Rachael talked about you a lot. She called you her 'big friend with the nice eyes.'" Melissa felt a lump in her throat. Laura continued, "I used to read to her at night when her mother couldn't stay. Even when I wasn't on duty, but just studying here in the hospital library, I'd stop by to see her." Laura smiled. "Rachael had a way of growing on you, didn't she?"

"Yes, she did." Melissa cleared her throat. "I didn't even know she was back in the hospital. The last time I saw her she seemed better."

Laura continued fluffing the pillow. "When it happens, it happens quickly."

"'It?'"

"Dying." Laura said the word solemnly.

Melissa dug her fingernails into her palms and turned to gaze at the monitors and machines. They were mute and indifferent. There was no life force for them to measure now. "Did she hurt before she died?"

"No. She was even a little excited. At first, she was afraid of going away. That's what her mother had told her—that she was going to a beautiful place where she could play and never hurt again. She wanted her mother to come with her, or at least one of the nurses."

"But, of course, no one could go with her." Melissa said the words absently. "It's something everyone has to do on her own."

"She slipped into a coma and died."

"Thank you for telling me. I'm sorry I didn't know sooner so I could have visited with her."

"There's a few of her things left in a bag," Laura said kindly. "I gathered them up to send to her family. Would you like to look through them?"

Laura handed her a plastic sack. She saw the teddy bear first, the one she'd given Rachael. It was worn in places, the fur rubbed off, and it was missing an eye. Its red felt tongue was half pulled out. "Looks like she loved it a lot," Laura observed.

Blinking furiously, Melissa sorted through papers with scribbles and pages from coloring books. She saw one of Prince Charming holding the glass slipper for Cinderella and her breath caught. "Do you think it would be all right if I kept this one? You see, I have the one of Cinderella in her ball gown, and . . ." Her voice cracked and Laura touched her shoulder.

"Take it. I'm sure it's fine."

With trembling fingers, Melissa folded the piece of paper and tucked it into her purse. She shivered. Rachael Dove had lived four short years and left behind a wounded teddy bear and a handful of colored papers. "Thank you." Her voice was barely audible. "I . . . I guess I should be going."

"Nice to meet you, Melissa."

When she reached the doorway she looked back at the room. Everything was there except Rachael, life. Yet Melissa knew that the child had left one more thing behind. She'd left an unforgettable memory of herself. Melissa ran down the hall to catch the elevator, tears coming in violent waves.

"Melissa! What are you doing here?" Ric stood so abruptly from the desk in his dorm room that his chair tipped over.

She closed the door behind her. "Are you alone?"

"Yeah, Doug's out with Cheri." He grabbed handfuls of clothes off his bed and shoved books and papers and soda cans out of the way to make a place for her to sit. "I thought you said you were getting together with Jory tonight."

Melissa paced, too restless to sit. "I went by the clinic this afternoon for lab work and then went up to the oncology floor."

"And?"

"And they told me that Rachael Dove had died."

He looked blank for a moment, then nodded. "The little girl you told me about. Gee, Melissa, I'm sorry. I know you liked her."

"I called my mom and told her I was eating out tonight, but really all I've been doing is driving around. And thinking."

Ric walked over to her and pulled her to his chest. "I'm glad you came to me, Melissa."

She leaned against him briefly, allowing one moment of softness and comfort to pass between them, then gently pulled away. "Maybe you won't be."

"Why?"

"I'm not going to Sarasota with you, Ric."

Stunned, he blinked. "Why not?"

She took her time answering, staring thoughtfully into space. "Before I got leukemia, I had so many plans. I wanted to make the Brain Bowl team—no junior has ever made the final panel. I wanted to be a National Merit Scholar. I wanted to go to college and study law. I wanted so many things, Ric."

"You were robbed," he said with a shrug. "We were both robbed. I wanted to run track."

"But I still want all those things, Ric. In spite of everything that's happened."

He reached for her, but she held up her hand to stop him. "What's that got to do with our spending the weekend together?"

Melissa searched for the right words to tell him what she felt. "You aren't my only option in life, Ric. Please don't make me your only one."

She saw anger in his eyes. "That doesn't make any sense. My life doesn't revolve around you."

"What does it revolve around?"

Agitated, he shoved his hands deep into the pockets of his jeans. "School. The fraternity. Things."

"But no track."

He scoffed. "Get real, Melissa. What kind of future does a one-legged runner have?"

"Make one. Be the first."

"You mean, 'If life gives you lemons, make lemonade'?" His tone was sarcastic. "Your romantic outlook is so sweet I could catch diabetes."

She laughed. "My brother calls me a hopeless romantic, too. And speaking of Michael, I thought of something else while I was driving around tonight."

Ric raked a hand through his hair and scowled, but he seemed resigned to listen, so Melissa continued. "When Michael was twelve he had a friend named Corley. I hated Corley's guts." She crossed her arms. "We'd always play board games at his house. Corley had every board game money could buy.

"Anyway, I began to notice that every time Michael or I began to win, Corley would make up a bunch of new rules. One day I got so mad, I wrecked up the board, called him some names, and stormed out of the house. Michael caught up with me and tried to calm me down. When I told Michael I was angry because Corley was cheating, you know what he said? He said, 'I know. But when someone changes the rules of the game, you either play by the new rules, or you don't play.'" She paused to let her statement sink in. "I remembered that tonight even though it happened years and years ago." She reached out and touched Ric's arm. "Ric, I didn't ask for cancer. Or for all the chemo and tests and hospital time. The rules of my life got changed, horribly changed. But I still want to play."

"And going to Sarasota with me, committing to me, isn't part of your game plan?" His question was bitter.

"No." A fine film of tears welled in her eyes. "But being asked was the nicest thing you could have done. You made me feel really good inside," she added shyly.

He stroked her cheek and let his fingers brush her wig. "I didn't do it to be nice."

"And that's what made it even more special. Because you cared. You really cared about me." She squeezed his hand and moved toward the door, until she felt the hard knob touch her spine. "Goodbye, Ric."

He started forward and stopped. "Melissa, if you ever change your mind . . ."

"You'll be the first to know." She closed the door behind her, then leaned against it for support. It was the hardest conversation she'd ever held, and it meant closing a chapter in her life that might never be opened again. She remembered the fire she'd felt when Ric had caressed her body.

"At least leukemia didn't dull your hormones," she told herself wryly under her breath. She left the dorm quickly and headed home, knowing that the next afternoon held one more giant hurdle for her to overcome.

Chapter Twenty

Melissa fidgeted with her belongings until every-one except the faculty advisors had left the Brain Bowl drill session. The names of the final panelists would be posted the next day, and Melissa knew deep down inside that her name wouldn't be on the list.

When the last student had left the room, Melissa took a deep breath and approached the teachers, who sat at a conference table comparing notes—Mrs. Watson, Mr. Marshall, Dean Crane, Mr. Wilson, and Miss Judd. She cleared her throat and they all looked up at her.

Mr. Marshall asked, "Did you want something, Melissa?"

With a calm voice that in no way reflected the panic she felt, she asked, "Would you please tell me now if I'm going to be on the panel or not?"

Mrs. Crane said, "Now, dear, that wouldn't be fair, would it? Everyone wants to know, and besides, that's what our meeting now is for—to decide."

Melissa gritted her teeth and refused to back down. "You aren't going to choose me, are you?"

The teachers exchanged glances. "We've made no decisions, Melissa," Mr. Wilson said, but without meeting her eyes.

Her stomach sank, like a fifty-foot drop on a roller coaster. Her suspicions were confirmed—they had no intentions of selecting her. "Why?" She asked.

"Why what?"

"Why won't you choose me?" Her anger fueled a boldness she didn't know she had. "I'm good at the game and you know it."

"You're the best," Mrs. Watson said, and received a sharp look from Mrs. Crane.

But the words buoyed Melissa. "I've worked harder than anyone. And my specialty is math. No one's quicker at solving problems than me. I'm always first on the buzzer with a math problem."

"Balance, Melissa," Miss Judd said. "We pick the team for balance."

Melissa straightened. "It's because of my cancer, isn't it? You're afraid that I'll get sick or something."

The quick exchange of looks between the advisors told her she'd guessed correctly. *Prejudice.* Isn't that what Mrs. Watson had tried to warn her about weeks before?

Mrs. Crane tapped her pencil on the table. "Melissa, your illness is a factor. You were out for such a long time . . ."

"But I've not missed one session since January. Not one!" She felt small tremors course through her body. "You have no right to hold that against me."

"If our team advances," Mr. Wilson said, "the pressure will be very intense. We can't afford to have a panelist drop off."

Mrs. Crane added quickly, "And you're just a junior, Melissa. You do have next year, you know."

Melissa crossed her arms and attacked their logic. "So in other words, I may be too sick to be on the panel this year, but not so sick that I won't be around to try again next year." From the corner of her eye, she saw Mrs. Watson slip her a thumbs-up signal. Encouraged, Melissa let the words tumble out. "Who of you can say, 'I'll be here next year'? Or next week? Nobody's tomorrows are a sure thing. If I make no plans for a future, then I'll never have a future. Don't you see? Don't you understand?"

The room had gone quiet, so quiet that Melissa could hear the clock on the wall when its hand jumped to pass another minute. Sweat trickled down between her shoulder blades. How had she ever found the guts to say those things to teachers?

Mr. Marshall cleared his throat, and his appraisal of her was both direct and pensive. "You're right, Melissa. You need to know right now if you'll be selected for the panel or not." He glanced down the row of startled faces. "I personally recruited Melissa last September because I thought she had what it took to participate in Brain Bowl. Nothing has happened over the past few months to change my opinion. I want her on the final panel."

"Me too," Mrs. Watson added emphatically.

Miss Judd nodded, then Mr. Wilson. Melissa's heart pounded. Mrs. Crane pressed her lips together, but finally offered a brief, terse nod. Melissa felt her legs trembling as Mr. Marshall stood and shook her hand. "Congratulations, Miss Austin. But please hold off telling anyone until all the names are posted tomorrow. All right?"

"It's a deal," she whispered, not trusting her voice to hold.

Mrs. Watson leaned forward. "By this time next year, you'll be a veteran. Imagine how strong we'll be when we have someone on the team two years in a row."

Two years in a row. Tomorrow. The future. Melissa flashed her a winning smile. "Yes, next year. When I'm a senior."

Chapter Twenty-one

Melissa slipped on the bright green jacket, smoothed her palms over the fine linen fabric, and examined the intricate green-and-gold Lincoln High School crest sewn on the breast pocket. Her bedroom mirror told her she looked every inch the exclusive representative of the Brain Bowl team that she felt she was.

With satisfaction she inspected her makeup, then her hair and figure. Gingerly, she touched the ends of her wig, smoothing them under, close to her ears. Few traces of her ordeal with leukemia remained, and unless someone had known her before, no one could tell she'd ever been sick. Yet, she cautioned her reflection, remission didn't mean the disease was over, but simply that it was held in check.

She thought about the night ahead of her. In two hours, she'd be sitting on the stage of the Tampa Civic Center Auditorium facing every other high school panel in the Bay area for round one of Brain Bowl. Butterflies fluttered in her stomach, but they were welcomed. Her nerves tingled, but they also felt sharp and alert. Melissa knew that she was ready for the competition.

She thought back to the week before, when the names had first been posted and read over the school PA system. All day long, kids had stopped her in the halls and congratulated her. And late in the afternoon, when she'd been waiting for Jory by her car, Brad had hailed her.

"Wait up, Melissa," he'd said, jogging toward her. He still had the power to make her heartbeat quicken, and she guessed some things would never change. "I'm really glad you made the team and I just wanted to say, congratulations and I told you so."

"Congratulations to you too, Brad. I'm glad they picked you to be captain. We're gonna win it, you know."

"Of course we're going to win it."

An April breeze ruffled her hair, blowing it across her cheek, and he reached out to smooth it. This time, Melissa did not withdraw from his touch. "The wind can't do much damage," she said, holding his gaze. "It's only a wig."

"I figured. I had an aunt who went through chemo, and she lost her hair and had to wear a wig, too."

Suddenly, she felt a jumble of hopes and illusions and wishes. She glanced at his wrist and noticed that the ID bracelet still belonged to Sarah. Then, setting her mind at ease, she let go of her longings for Brad. She slugged him playfully on the arm. "My real hair's growing out well, and by the end of the summer, I'll bet it's past my jawline."

"I'll check you out before I go away to college," he told her. They talked for a few minutes and she watched him head toward his car. Now, days later, Melissa could really shrug off the last vestiges of yearning, and refocus her energy on the evening ahead.

There was a knock at her door and Jory breezed in, her green eyes dancing. "All set?"

"What do you think?" Melissa twirled, showing off the jacket, white pleated skirt, and white pumps.

"Preppy," Jory said, then added with an impish smile, "but on you, it's sensational."

"You look different," Melissa observed, scrutinizing her friend from head to toe. Jory's standard funky look had been replaced by polished sophistication. Her dress was simple, but elegant, the green perfect for her auburn hair. Her usual wild shade of nail polish had been exchanged for a soft shade of apricot.

Self-consciously, Jory dropped her gaze. "I decided it was time for a new image. Even Peter Pan had to grow up."

"I'll bet Michael will approve."

"Do you think so?"

Jory asked the question so quickly and with such eagerness that Melissa intuitively reached out and squeezed her friend's hands. "Let's go dazzle him with our combined beauty. I'll bet he and Mom are waiting for our grand entrance right now."

Jory hung back slightly. "In a minute. First, I want to give you a present."

Melissa noticed the small bag Jory was holding. Surprised, she asked, "For me? What is it?"

"Close your eyes." Melissa obeyed, more excited than curious. "Okay, open them."

Jory held a wig, a fall of hair that was rich and black and incredibly long. Melissa stared, open-mouthed. "Oh, Jory . . ."

"It's *real* hair, Melissa," Jory began to babble. "I sent for it ages ago, through a salon in New York that specializes in only the finest. I sent them pictures of you and had them make up the hairpiece just for you. It's just like your real hair, don't you think, Melissa? I insisted that it had to be perfect. Tell me you like it. Tell me you'll wear it."

Mesmerized, Melissa reached out and touched the hair, sifting it through her fingers. Tears gathered on her lashes. "I-It must have cost a fortune . . ."

Jory dismissed her remark with an impatient wave. "It's my money and I can spend it however I like."

Unable to take her eyes off the hair, Melissa whispered. "Help me put it on."

In moments the switch was accomplished and Melissa could only stare in the mirror at the reborn image of herself. "I-I'd almost forgotten . . ." She gathered a fistful of the hair and rolled it through her fingers, feeling the luxurious weight of it, the silkiness of it on her skin. It hung to her waist and she tossed her head to feel the way it brushed her shoulders and flowed down her back. She caught Jory's eyes in the mirror and turned toward her. "Thank you."

Jory blinked, haphazardly running her forefinger beneath an eye. "Don't want to smear my mascara," she mumbled, shifting nervously from foot to foot.

Without a word, Melissa slipped her arms around Jory and hugged her tightly, not caring that she herself was crying and probably ruining her own carefully applied makeup. "It's the most beautiful gift I've ever been given. I love you, Jory Delaney."

"Oh, Melissa, I love you, too. You're my best friend. My *best*."

Melissa might never have let Jory go, except for a rap on her door and Michael's muffled, impatient voice. "Aren't you two ready yet? We're going to be late if you don't light a fire under yourselves."

"Cool out. We're coming," Melissa said. Both

girls quickly touched up their makeup, then Melissa opened the door with an exaggerated flair. "Good grief, Michael, I can tell time and we're not late."

When he saw her he stared, shocked. "It's a gift from Jory," she told him.

He looked at Jory, standing timidly behind Melissa, who stepped aside. "You did this for Melissa?" he asked.

Jory tilted her head, her expression caught between defiance and desperation. "Why not? What are friends for?"

Michael's hand drifted up to touch Jory's cheek. "Thank you," he said. He tipped her chin upward and with incredible tenderness said again, "Thank you, Jory." She blushed, staring into Michael's eyes, unable to speak.

Reluctantly Melissa broke the spell. "Are we ready?"

Michael stepped away from Jory and took Melissa's hand. "Mom's waiting in the car."

Melissa's heart swelled, and she was filled with joy. "Last one out buys milk shakes for everyone after the match," she called. "Chocolate!"

She bounded out of the room and down the stairs, her hair chasing behind her. It caught the lamp glow and sparkled like starlight in the night.

ABOUT THE AUTHOR

LURLENE MCDANIEL has been a professional writer for more than twenty years and has written radio and television scripts, promotional and advertising copy, and a magazine column. She began writing inspirational novels about life-altering situations for children and young adults after one of her sons was diagnosed with juvenile diabetes. She lives in Chattanooga, Tennessee.

Lurlene McDaniel's popular Bantam Starfire books include *Goodbye Doesn't Mean Forever,* the companion novel to *Too Young to Die, Somewhere Between Life and Death, Time to Let Go,* and *Now I Lay Me Down to Sleep.*

Lurlene McDaniel loves to hear from her fans. You can write to her % Bantam Books, 666 Fifth Avenue, New York, NY 10103. If you would like a response, please include a self-addressed stamped envelope.